USA TODAY BESTSELLING AUTHOR

SKYE MACKINNON

Cover by MiblArt.

Formatting by Gina Wynn.

Illustration of Blaze the unicorn by Warlocklord.

Published by Peryton Press.

skyemackinnon.com

Contents

To the Flock – this book wouldn't exist without you

What Happened Before

Wyn, heiress to the Winter throne, slayer of demons, etc, was slowly getting used to life in her mother's Palace. Except for the dresses, she's never going to get used to those.

She met Blaze, a unicorn, learned to fly and went on some dates with her Guardians (finally!). But of course, something had to happen to destroy all of that. She got poisoned, almost died, ended up in the Library of Lives where she had to prove that she was worthy of becoming Immortal.

Back in the Realm, she had to deal with the dragon shifter who'd tried to kill her, but he refused to say anything, not even when the Guardian Ada questioned him. He'd taken poison which turned out to be made from a plant only found in the Demon Realms, which led the Council to wonder whether their main suspect, the Summer God Angus, might be working with the demons.

Wyn finally confronted Crispin about his past, and he showed her some of his memories of how he was created by the Morrigan and turned into her assassin and torturer.

Wyn had been worried about her adoptive parents for a long time, so she managed to persuade Arc to find a way to check on them. With the help of a demon, they created a mental link and were able to speak through the demon as he visited Wyn's parents. Well, never trust a demon. He kidnapped her parents, telling them that he was doing it for the Morrigan.

At a Council meeting to discuss the situation, a messenger suddenly brought in a box. Inside it was the hand of Wyn's adoptive mum, and when Wyn touched it, she saw that her mother was dead and her father still prisoner of the Morrigan.

In a bit of a mental breakdown, she decided to become like Beira, an ice queen without emotion.

In the epilogue, the demoness Chesca appears at one of the Realm's Gates, asking to speak to Wyn. She gets killed by one of the guards, but manages to give them her final message: that the Morrigan is behind it all and that she controls the demons.

The People of the Realm

Family

Wyn, demi-goddess and heroine of this series
Her Guardians: Storm, Frost, Arc and Crispin
Beira, the Queen of Winter and Wyn's mother
James, Wyn's adoptive father
Rose, Wyn's adoptive mother

The Council

Gwain, Master of Arms
Ada, Gwain's second-in-command
Tamara, Mistress of the Household (and spy mistress)
Algonquin, Librarian
Zephyr, Master of the Wings
Theodore, Healer
Magnus, Treasurer

Friends

Blaze, unicorn extraordinaire
Chesca, demoness (deceased)
Aodh, Chesca's lover (deceased)

Enemies

Angus, Summer King
Bridget, his wife
Morrigan, Goddess of Death
Demons... well, they're evil

Chapter One

They say grief passes. They say the pain gets less.

Well, I don't want it to go. I don't want it to stop hurting.

The pain helps me function and get through the day. And it helps me focus on one thing: revenge.

Mum. Chesca. And we don't know if my dad is still alive.

I wish I could say that I'd feel it if he was dead, but I'm so empty inside that I don't think I would. I don't feel much, anymore. It's all shards and fragments inside my heart, nothing but a broken mess.

The only thing that can make me feel even a tiny bit alive is Blaze's unicorn dust. Sparklies, as he calls it. I touch his horn and feel better. For a while, at least. My Guardians have been trying to stop me from going to him, but I just push them away or evade them. I need to forget, at least once a day. What else is there otherwise but death and despair?

It's been a week now since that dreadful day. There's nothing for me to do. My mother is talking to her allies, her fellow Gods and Goddesses, while the Master of Arms is readying his troops. My men are busy doing the same, preparing for the coming battle.

But there won't be a battle if we don't find the Morrigan first. She's still in the shadows, still hiding. How can we fight a phantom?

As there's nothing for me to do, I have too much time to think. Too much time to remember.

Blaze is the only one who seems to be listening to me. Who doesn't ask stupid questions, like 'how are you'. Want to know how I am? Fucking dreadful. I'm a hollow shell propelled by revenge. That's all that's keeping me going. Otherwise I'd lie curled up in my bed.

Not that I haven't done that as well. I've spent a lot of time in my bedroom, staring at the ceiling, ignoring the servants trying to come in and bring me food. I use magic to lock the doors so that nobody can disturb me. Not even my men.

I no longer care about food. If someone gives me something, I eat it, but I no longer feel hungry.

My mum, my beautiful mum. I can't get her pain out of my head. How the Morrigan sliced off her arm. How she put a knife in my mother's heart. That all-encompassing pain that killed her. It replays over and over in my head. Not images; it was too dark in that dungeon to see much. Just the emotions, my mum's fear, her pain, my father's anguish. It never stops, it's running constantly like a loop, driving me crazy.

And the image of her severed hand... only one thing gets that out of my head.

I step into the hole that leads to Blaze's home and wait for the magic elevator to transport me to the bottom. My head is aching a little, but I know that the pain will disappear once I have my sparklies. It always does. And at least the physical pain in my skull is easier to bear than the mental pain assaulting me every minute of every day.

"Welcome back," Blaze greets me. He's spread out on a large purple cushion, his front legs folded underneath his body. His white fur looks as pristine as always and his horn is glittering slightly. My mouth waters at the thought of the sparklies that are awaiting me. Not that they're something to eat, but sparklies still feel like nourishment.

I don't waste time on small talk. Blaze knows why I'm here. I don't care about how he is or what he's been up to since I last saw him yesterday afternoon. I approach him and touch his horn without further ado.

Bliss fills me. Happiness is next. I sink to the ground, smiling widely as the familiar warm feeling spreads in my chest, drowning out the darkness in there. My thoughts turn fuzzy and I sigh in relief. I'm almost there. That moment when everything disappears and all my memories fade. That moment when I can live in the present, unaffected by what happened in the past. That moment when I can simply be, without sadness, without the cold that is surrounding my heart, without the guilt I carry deep within me.

The sparklies are flowing through my body, gently warming me all over. They're soft and lovely. I want to feel them all the time. I don't want it to stop. Everything is so pretty now. Blaze is twinkling all over, his cave is shimmering and even my hands are full of rainbow glitter. Life is so beautiful when reality slips away.

As always, it's over far too soon. The happiness ends without warning and darkness returns, clinging onto my heart. The room turns cold and unfriendly.

No, I need more. I don't want this emptiness. I need colour in my life.

"Give me more," I beg Blaze and reach for his horn, but he turns away before I can touch it. I stumble to my feet and stagger towards him, but he's moving away from me, looking at me strangely.

"Princess..." he mutters, but he continues to retreat.

No. I want more. He's one of my subjects, he has to do what I want him to.

"Come here," I order and his eyes widen.

He looks tempted to step forward, but then he shakes his head. "No, you're not my Queen. I won't give you any more, this has been going on long enough."

I growl in frustration and stumble towards him, but for every step I take, he manages to take two back. This isn't going to work, I'm too unsteady on my feet.

With a groan, I reach for my magic. I don't care about what kind of power I draw from it, I just fling it at Blaze, willing him to stand still for me.

He whinnies in fear as a circle of flames bursts into existence around him. Usually, this would make me stop, but my heart is ice and even the scared look in his eyes doesn't reach it. The flames are reflecting in his dark, wide pupils.

This time, he doesn't move when I approach him. He's frozen in shock, or maybe because he'll get burnt if he even takes a single step in any direction. Finally, I get to reach for his horn and touch it – at the same time as the flames take hold of my sleeve and begin to eat it up.

Bliss and happiness fill the emptiness inside of me, mixed with a pain that I can't quite place. Usually there's no pain when I go into the beautiful world of sparklies. Maybe this will be a new, good experience? Sometimes there's pleasure in pain.

I sink to the ground, my mind slowly retreating and becoming slow. Calm. Non-existent.

The pain is still there though and it's preventing me from letting go completely. It's getting stronger.

I curl up into a ball, thinking that might make the pain go away. Sometimes hiding from the world works. Not this time, though.

The bliss is pushed away and more pain crashes into me. I scream in agony.

I could open my eyes to see what's causing it, but the sparklies won't let me. They're still inside of me, but while they usually make me happy, today they seem to increase the pain.

It's getting worse and worse and I can't stop screaming.

There's another scream, an echo perhaps, maybe someone else. I dimly remember Blaze being there. Maybe he's screaming to make fun of me?

"What the fuck is going on here – oh no, Wyn!"

Voices, curses, shouting.

I'm thrown into a pool of water. No, water is thrown on me. Or both? It's hard to tell. At least it makes my mind a little clearer. Enough to know that the voice talking rapidly in the background is Frost.

A moment later, I wish my head wasn't clearing. Red hot pain flares up in my right arm, all the way up to my shoulder and neck. It hurts so much, please, make it stop. I whimper and someone grips my left hand and squeezes it reassuringly.

"Shush, Crispin will be here soon," Frost whispers and more water runs over me, cooling my hot skin a little. "What did you do to yourself, Wyn? No, don't try to move. Blaze is getting Crispin, they won't be long."

I'm having trouble keeping up with what he's saying. Crispin? Why do I need Crispin? Oh, the pain, maybe because of that? Crispin heals, maybe he can heal me. The pain in my body and in my mind. And then I can get some more sparklies from Blaze to make me forget about it all.

The water that's been running over my skin disappears and immediately, the pain gets worse.

"Don't stop," I whimper hoarsely.

"Okay, but let me know if you get cold."

The water returns and cools my burning skin. It doesn't make the pain go away, but it softens it slightly. It gives me another sensation to focus on, one that's cooler and nicer than the aches.

"Frost," I whisper.

"Yes, Wyn?"

"It hurts."

I think about what I just said for a moment, then I add, "I don't want to whine."

He chuckles sadly. "Whine as much as you want. It's better than keeping up that façade you've been showing us. Let it all out."

"What?" I'm confused. My mind is still muddled with both the pain and the sparklies.

"You're grieving. You need to let us in, Wyn, or it's going to eat you up from the inside."

"The pain is outside," I mutter, noticing how it seems to be getting worse. The water is no longer taking the edge off like it did before.

"Now, yes, but that's not what I'm talking about." He gently strokes my face but I'm not sure I like the feeling. It's too close, too intense.

"Let's have this conversation when you're better. Crispin will be here soon, and he'll make you feel better. Then we can go back to the Palace and you can rest."

"Sleep sounds good," I croak, "but without the pain."

There's a rumbling far away, then footsteps, fast and getting closer.

"What happened?"

"Let me through!"

"I'm going to kill that unicorn."

Someone kneels by my side, but I whimper when they touch my side.

"It's okay, it's me, Crispin." His voice is soothing, gentle, and I want to sink into it, drifting away. But the pain isn't letting me.

"Those burns are bad. I'll make you fall asleep so I can work on them, is that okay?"

I shake my head and groan at the pain of it. "No. No sleep."

Sleep brings nightmares. Memories. Feelings.

I hate sleeping.

"Arc, come here! Can you put her into one of your trances? Healing her will hurt, I don't want her to be awake for that."

A hand lowers onto my forehead, cool and warm at the same time. "Of course. Wyn, relax. It'll all be over soon. Let me in, lower your barriers. There won't be any dreams, I promise. No nightmares. Just rest."

With all the sparklies in my blood, my barriers are already down, but before I can tell him, I slip away, out of my body, into something peaceful.

No more pain.

Chapter Two

A double rainbow is beckoning on the horizon. Two perfect arcs, parallel to each other, touching the earth on both ends.

"Beautiful, isn't it?"

I turn around and face Arc. He's smiling widely as he turns his gaze away from the rainbow and looks straight at me.

"Welcome ta my safe place."

"Where are we?" I ask, looking down at ourselves. Arc is wearing a grey kilt and a white shirt, but besides that, he's barefoot. We're standing on bright green grass, far too colourful to be real. It's soft under my naked feet and I curl my toes into the warm earth. I'm wearing a simple blue dress, one I've never seen before. Even though I don't usually like dresses, this one is surprisingly comfortable.

"In my mind. This is where I come when I need some peace and quiet."

"You let me into your mind?"

He shrugs. "Ye already have my heart, why not my mind? Ye needed a place ta recover, ta escape while Crispin does his healing. This seemed as good a space as any."

I remember now. The pain, the fire, the sparklies.

"What happened exactly?"

He grimaces. "I'm not quite sure, but it looked like ye set yerself on fire. Yer shirt caught fire as well, and yer hair... I'm sorry."

"What about my hair?"

He looks uncomfortable. "Ehm, there wasn't much left on one side."

I gingerly touch my head, but my hair feels as it always does, falling just below my shoulders on both sides.

"This isn't real," Arc explains. "Ye're seeing yerself like ye want to, not like ye look right now in reality."

"So when I wake up, I'll be bald?" I ask, not quite sure what to think of that. My mind is still processing it all.

"Only on one side, I think." He gives me a little grin. "Ye could turn it into a mohawk, shock the Court a wee bit."

I smile at the thought of Algonquin or Theodore seeing me like that. Maybe a punk style would be a clear sign for them all to leave me alone. Ignoring them or giving them glares didn't work.

"Finally!" Arc explains, looking at me joyfully.

"What?"

"Ye smiled. That's the first time in eight days that ye've smiled."

Immediately, I put my mask back into place, erasing that traitorous smile.

Arc's expression darkens. "Ye're allowed ta smile, Princess. Please dinnae lock yerself away again."

I shake my head, trying to ignore his sad look. "I can't. How can I smile when my mother is dead, her body dismembered somewhere? How can I smile when I don't know where my father is, if he's alive, even?"

Arc puts his hands on my shoulders and even though I can barely stand the touch, I stay where I am, looking down at the ground, willing my tears to disappear.

"Neither of them would want ye to be all cold like that," Arc says softly. "Just because that's how Queen Beira rules, doesn't mean that ye should be the same. Come back to us, Wyn. Dinnae stay in that darkness. Let us in."

If I was my normal self, I'd hug him and tell him that everything was going to be alright. But I'm not. The Wyn he knows is locked away inside of me and I have no intention of letting her out. She's not strong enough for this new world. I have to be cold and unfeeling to survive. I can't break down, I need to keep going. Why can't they understand that? Why do they try and make me let down my barriers?

No, I can't.

I shrug off his hands and step back, before slamming up my walls. The rainbows disappear, then everything else goes black and I'm thrown back into my body.

Bye, Arc. I'm sorry.

Pain welcomes me with open arms. I don't fight it. I deserve it.

I let myself enjoy the warmth of the Guardian holding me for just a moment before opening my eyes. Crispin is bent over my body, his hands running close over my skin without actually touching me. He's not noticed yet that I'm awake.

The pain is almost more than when I was burning. Whatever he's doing isn't gentle. But that's good. I let my parents down, I brought the demon into their house. My mum is dead because of me. This pain isn't punishment enough.

"Wyn," Arc groans, holding his head. He's sitting on the floor next to me, his back against the wall. His face is pale beneath his red hair.

"What happened?" Storm asks worriedly and kneels beside his fellow Guardian.

"She pushed me away," Arc sighs, pointing at me.

Crispin looks up from his work and his eyes widen when he sees that I'm awake.

"Shit, you weren't supposed to be conscious while I'm doing this. That's it. You're going to sleep."

"No," I whisper, my voice rough from pain and smoke.

"You had your chance," Storm growls angrily. "Crisp, put her to sleep. Then once you've healed her, we're going home. No more sparklies."

"But I need them..."
Sleep rushes at me and I'm gone before I can fight it.

"What are we going to do now?" Frost whispers. His voice is almost too far to hear but he's in the same room.

"From now on, one of us stays with her at all times." That's Storm, not my lover Storm, but the leader, the serious one. "When she tries to go to Blaze, stop her. Not that the unicorn will give her any more, he's learned his lesson. I don't think he expected her to get addicted as quickly as she did."

"He should be grateful I healed him," Crispin growls. "He'd be dead if Frost hadn't been shadowing them."

"What if she tries ta leave? We cannae stop her, she's the Princess."

"We've sworn to protect her," Storm says gravely. "Even if that means protecting her from herself. I'm sure Her Majesty agrees, but if she doesn't, I'll take it on me to deal with the consequences."

"She pushed me away," Arc mutters, his voice full of sadness. "She's never done that before."

Storm sighs. "She's not herself at the moment. She's grieving, she's in an unfamiliar place and she wants revenge. It's not a good place for anyone to be in. She needs time, but I'm not sure how much we can give her. The war is coming and we need to be prepared."

I don't need time. I'm ready for war. Ready to crush the Morrigan. I've secured my heart, protecting it from further injuries. I don't know if my father is still alive. If he isn't... I can't crash. I need to continue fighting. I can't let feelings hold me back. That was the old Wyn, but she was weak. To defeat the Goddess of Death, I will need my mind, not my heart.

"I'm worried we're losing her," Arc whispers. "I've never seen her barriers so strong. She's keeping us oot, what if she never lets us in again?"

He sounds so forlorn, so sad that I want to give him a hug - no, that's the old Wyn. Stop it. Hugging doesn't help anyone. It's just a waste of time and energy.

"Remember, we're bound to her," Crispin says soothingly, but even he sounds a little unsure. "Eventually, she won't be able to fight the bond any longer. She needs us just as much as we need her."

I can't take it any longer and move my arms and legs, stretching as if I'm only just waking up.

"Good morning, Princess."

A smiling Frost is the first I see when I open my eyes.

"How are you feeling?"

"Fine. What time is it?"

His smiles wavers a little. "Almost noon. The healing took a lot of your own energy so we let you sleep..."

I jump out of bed, not letting him finish. So much time wasted. I need to consult with my mother, then a quick trip to Blaze, then there's likely a Council meeting, then...

Wait, Blaze.

"Is he alright?"

"Who? The unicorn?" Storm sneers in disapproval.

"Yes, who else," I reply impatiently. "Did he get hurt?"

"He's fine," Frost says, walking around me until he's standing in my way. His eyes are soft and warm, but there's a question in there, a plea for me to respond to him. Not to his words, to his feelings.

I turn my head, unable to look at the want in his eyes. I can't give him what he needs.

"Crispin healed him after he was done with you," Frost explains, hurt swinging in his voice. "But he's left for a little while, until-"

I swirl around and grab Frost by the shoulders, almost shaking him.

"Why would he leave? Where did he go?"

Frost looks down, evading my eyes.

"He had something to do..."

I squeeze his arms tighter.

"But I need him." My voice isn't as strong as I'd like it to be, in fact, it's almost a whimper. No more sparklies. I need them. I can't go on without them. Blaze is the only one who can make me forget, who takes the edge off the pain. Without him, I'll have to live in the cold and the dark, the way the world has been feeling ever since the day the box arrived. My mother's...

No, don't think of that. Don't let it get close to you. They were your adoptive parents, not your real ones. Her death isn't as bad as it seems. Beira is your real mother. She's still alive, she needs you.

"I need them..." This time, it really is a whimper.

My breathing is getting faster but I can't control it; it's my body who's taken over. My legs shake and I slowly sink to the floor, clinging to whatever's closest.

I can't do this.

I'm not strong enough. I can't shield my emotions well enough. Sometimes they need to be let out, and I can only do that with Blaze. He doesn't judge, he doesn't tell anyone. With him I can be happy for a few moments every day, before the darkness takes over once more.

"Shush, Wyn, it'll be alright."

A hand rubs my back soothingly and it's grating against my barriers.

No, I can't.

I wiggle free from their touch and stumble to my feet. Everything is spinning and I'm vaguely aware that my breathing is far too fast, but I need to get away from them. They're too nice, too kind. I can't give them what they want.

Surprisingly, I reach the bathroom before any of them can stop me. I turn the key in the lock and then sink down to the ground again, leaning against the cool wooden door.

Blaze has abandoned me, just when I needed him most. I thought I could trust the unicorn.

I hug my knees to my chest. My heart is close to breaking free but I can't let that happen. I need to keep it in its icy prison, even if it hurts. I need to keep functioning. But why is it all so difficult?

It's the men. They're making it harder. Without them, all I'd have to worry about was myself. But even now I can feel my connection to them, the bond pulling us towards each other. If I gave in, I'd open the door and throw myself into their arms.

The bond is getting more demanding with every day I don't touch my Guardians. I never noticed before how often I touched them. A slight brush against each other on a corridor, a quick kiss on the way to a meeting, cuddling in bed before falling asleep in their arms. Even if it wasn't always all of them together, there was usually one of them around. And now that I'm keeping them at a distance, the bond is making me suffer for it.

Damn those Guardians for making me go through with that ritual. Maybe the connection we had before, the one created by them syphoning some of my magic, wouldn't have been strong enough to keep us together. Maybe I could have made them leave. But with the other bond, that's impossible.

A knock on the door sends tiny vibrations through my spine.

"Wyn, are you alright?"

I ignore Storm and draw my legs closer. Not that it makes me feel any better.

He knocks again, harder this time. The entire door shakes and with a sigh, I get up, looking for a better place to sit.

That's when I see myself in the mirror. I shriek before I can stifle the scream with my hands.

It isn't me.

It can't be.

The Wyn in the mirror is staring back at me, wide-eyed, her singed eyebrows giving her a strangely confused look.

With a crash, the door flies open.

"What's-?"

Storm doesn't finish his question. He knows exactly what's wrong.

Half of my hair is gone. My scalp is an ugly red, the skin puckered where the hair used to be. My hair is normal on the left side, but then as soon as it reaches the parting, it turns into a strange lightning bolt shape, leaving a few tufts at the front with a giant bald batch just behind.

I gingerly touch the back of my head. Again, there's no hair left on the right side.

"I healed you, but I couldn't regrow your hair," Crispin says softly. I didn't even notice him entering the room. "Maybe your mother can. Or we can get you a wig, or a pretty headscarf, or..."

"Get out!" I scream and blast them with a burst of wind, shooting out of me before I can stop it. Crispin is flung against the wall with a crack, while the door slams against Storm. Both of them cry out in pain and I freeze, watching as Crispin slumps to the floor, blood staining the wall where his head crashed against it.

The door opens again and in comes a furious Storm, holding his bleeding nose.

"What the fuck are you playing at?" he shouts, stalking towards me. Frost and Arc are behind him, staring at me with grim faces.

"Crispin!" Frost has seen Crispin on the floor and hurries to kneel by his friend's side. "Crisp, can you hear me?"

He checks for a pulse while I wring my hands, ice flooding my veins. What have I done?

I begin to shiver, then my body starts to shake ever so slightly. The ice is reaching my heart, already cold, but it's a different kind of ice now. The current layer is one I put there myself. The new ice is one out of my control.

It scares me. Everything scares me.

Crispin groans and Frost sighs in relief. Arc is kneeling on Crispin's other side, but I didn't even notice him move. The world around me has turned into a dream that I'm watching, but not taking part in.

"Wyn?" Storm asks from far away, coming closer. The blood flowing from his nose has stopped, leaving brown traces behind. "Wynter?"

He never uses my full name. Why is he now?

Something is building up in me, a pressure that is starting somewhere near my heart. An icy energy is running through me and my shakes are getting stronger.

"Wyn, your eyes are glowing."

Are they? How strange.

Fog is clouding my mind and it's hard to stay focussed.

Something tickles my hand and I look down. Tiny sparks of lightning are sizzling around my fingers, so beautiful and pretty. I raise my hand to take a closer look, watching as the sparks are turning into larger bolts.

"Wyn, stop it!"

But why would I stop such a pretty thing? It's like Blaze's sparkly cave, only brighter and more powerful.

"Frost, get Crisp out of here. Everybody out, she's going to flare again!"

Storm is looking at me strangely, like he's afraid.

Is there something dangerous with us in the room? I look around, but there's nothing behind me. No monsters, no enemies.

"Wyn, you need to control your magic," Storm says, urgency lacing each of his words. "Without Crispin, we won't be able to contain it."

The intensity of his voice makes me stop and think, but I'm not sure how to use my magic anymore. It's too slippery, too powerful.

"Get out," I whisper with difficulty. Forming words is difficult. Holding on to reality is hard. I just want to let go, but Storm needs to get away from me first.

I expect him to refuse, but he gives me a quick nod and leaves the room.

"I'm going to get your mother!" he calls as he runs away.

Finally, I can let go.

Lightning burst from my body, crashing into my mind, making everything go blank.

Chapter Three

I wake up in an unfamiliar place. Not a bad place, though.

Shelves laden with books tower above me, reaching all the way up to a high ceiling. The air smells of parchment and ink; that beautiful scent you get when you open an old book.

I sit up and look around. It seems that I'm in a library of sorts, or an archive. Those shelves are enormous. They're higher than a house, and every inch of them is packed with books and scrolls. Some books look like they're about to fall apart, others are brand new.

"And who do we have here?" someone asks, his voice rough from age.

I stand and turn around, facing an old man with the longest beard I've ever seen. It reaches beyond his belt, falling in white, smooth curls. If he wasn't thin and lanky, he could be the spitting image of how most children imagine Father Christmas.

Bright green eyes look at me through thick glasses, sitting precariously on the very tip of his nose. He's smiling at me and I immediately have a good feeling about him. It's an honest, true smile.

"Who are you?" I ask in return and his smile widens.

"Where are my manners! I'm the Librarian."

I frown. "Don't you have a real name?"

"I do, but it doesn't matter. I'm the Librarian, and that's all there is to it. Now, who are you, if you don't mind me asking?"

His smile is turning cheeky, as if he's playing with me.

"Wyn... ehm, Wynter. Where exactly am I?"

"Look around you. Isn't it obvious?"

I voice the suspicion I had since I woke up.

"Am I in the Library of Lives again?"

He gives me an approving nod. "You are indeed. Shall I give you the tour?"

I'm still looking around in wonder. For someone like me, this is paradise. The Palace Library is nothing compared to this.

"I've been in the Library of Lives before, but it looked very different. More... like an office."

He chuckles. "You were in the administration wing. This here is the heart of the Library, the place where everything comes together. Come, I'll show you."

He walks along the narrow corridor, expecting me to follow. Still a bit dazed, I hurry to keep up with his long strides. I'm breathing in the beautiful smell of old books and with every breath, my heart gets a little lighter. This place is amazing. A dream come true.

"The library is formed like a circle with twenty spokes. We're in the dark ages spoke just now, so let's go to something more modern. Although I love reading about the lives of some of the people back then," he says, looking wistfully at one of the books we pass.

"How many books are there?" I ask, having a hard time imagining that there are books from centuries ago.

The Librarian shrugs. "I've never counted, and new ones are added each day. Whenever a child is born, a new book is created. The Library makes space for them, and somehow, it lets us find what we need."

I let that sink in for a moment, before asking, "Does that mean every person has a book in here?"

"Didn't I just say that?"

"Yes, but... there are billions of people. How can all those books fit into one room, even one as large as this?"

He laughs. "You're thinking in human terms. Here, everything is possible. The Library isn't human, it's so much more than that. Every person who's ever lived has a book here, and they're all in this room. Tell me someone random and I'll prove it to you."

"Wolfgang Amadeus Mozart." No idea why I picked my favourite composer, but for this, I suppose he's as good as any.

We finally reach the end of the Dark Ages spoke and enter a circular space with a round table in the middle, surrounded by leather chairs. On the table are heaps of old-fashioned index cards, some of them scribbled on, others unused. Pens are lying all around, giving the impression that usually, people are working here.

The Librarian takes an empty card and writes Mozart with a flourishing script onto it. The writing glows silver for a moment, then a new line of text appears.

He notices my confused look and gives me a smile. "It saves us from having to search entire spokes. The Library tells us where to go. It's rather ingenious."

Without further explanation, he walks around the table and enters a new corridor of shelves, and I have to almost run to keep up with his large strides. It doesn't take long for him to stop and look at a dark mahogany shelf board. Just like all the others, it's bending under the weight of the books tightly stashed on top of it.

He glides a finger along the spines of the books until he finds the one he's looking for. It's a red tome, bound in thick leather.

On the spine, Mozart's name is embossed in gold.

He hands me the book and looks at me expectantly.

"Open it."

I do as he asks, turning the first page with anticipation. It only states the years of his life, 1756 to 1791, but as soon as I turn the next page, it gets more interesting.

Day 1: Birth. A very unpleasant affair. Got to meet my parents and older sister.

Day 2: Christening. I cried a lot when the water touched my head.

What the...

"Is this for real?" I ask the Librarian, who's peeking over my shoulder, reading what I just read.

"It very much is, yes. We all write our books of life in a different way. Some write it like a diary, others are like biographies in the third person. Some don't contain any words, but drawings. Skip a few years ahead."

I turn about fifty pages and suddenly, the sentences turn into music. Mozart no longer thinks in words, but in musical notes. I flick through the pages, in awe of his work. There are entire symphonies in this book.

"Is this the music he wrote, or something else entirely?"

The Librarian strokes his long beard. "Both, I believe. I recognise a few of the pieces of music in there, but a lot aren't familiar to me at all. It's an astonishing book, certainly. A lot easier to read than that of Pythagoras, or," he shudders, "Kafka."

"Is it only the important people who have books here?"

He frowns. "Child, didn't you listen? Everybody has a book in the Library, from the most nondescript peasant to the greatest kings. Gods, too. There is nobody, alive or dead, who doesn't have their book in this room."

"Even you?"

"Even me. Although we're not allowed to look at our own books. They're hidden from us, so I've never even seen mine."

"Aren't you tempted to read it?"

He chuckles. "Why? I prefer to live my life, rather than read about it afterwards. Living in the present is much more important than doing deeds to be admired for in the future. Not that anybody would ever admire me. I'm just the Librarian."

Somehow, I know that he is a lot more than just the caretaker of this Library. He's got an air around him that reminds me of that of a God. Is there a God of Books? I'll need to ask my mother.

Which makes me think...

"Does my mother have one?"

"Of course, but it's under lock and key. Beira's life, knowledge and experiences are far too dangerous for people to read. If you want to look at it, you'll have to ask her permission. But before you do that, ask yourself, would you want anyone to read your own book?"

It doesn't take me long to think about that. No, of course not. It's too personal. Maybe once I'm dead, but even then... And besides, I'm kind of Immortal now. Which begs the question, why I'm in the Library now. I thought only dead people came here. But I passed all the tests the last time I was here, I shouldn't be dead.

How did I not ask this when I woke up?

Oh yes, the books distracted me. Books tend to do that.

"Am I dead?" I ask him bluntly, and the Librarian smiles at me benevolently. He's got something grandfatherly about him, something that makes me want to hug him.

"Only if you choose to be," he says mysteriously.

"Why would I choose to be?"

"Some Immortals get tired of living, so sometimes, they get to choose whether they want to continue their lives or pass on. That is the only time we are allowed to look in our own books - the time we make the decision between life and death. Of course, mortals don't get to make that decision, so they'll never even know these books exist."

I feel bad for my adoptive parents, my friends, hell, everybody I knew on Earth. They're living in a world without magic, one that I used to be in but which now feels very far away.

"Does that mean I died and can be revived if I choose to?" I ask him, trying to make sense of it all.

"No, you haven't died. Not yet, anyway. For now, time is frozen at the exact point where you could die."

His eyes unfocus for a moment, then his sharp gaze returns.

"There was an explosion, right?"

I nod. "I think my magic flared. I don't really remember."

"It's about to collapse part of the Royal Palace. Your mother is transporting all the people out of it, but your barriers are up and she cannot reach you. Your choice is simple: let her save you or die."

"My Guardians are safe?"

He smiles indulgently.

"Everybody is safe. You're not deciding about anybody else's life. Just your own."

I'm struggling to think of a reason why I wouldn't want to live. I'm happy, right? I have four loving men, I'm healthy, I have my parents...

Wait.

It's as if I'm suddenly doused in cold water.

How could I forget? My mum is dead. My father a prisoner of the Morrigan.

I'm not happy. I was sad, so terribly alone and filled with hate.

Those emotions are only echoes now; this place is filtering out all the negative feelings and leaving just the good ones. Almost like Blaze's sparklies, but less fake. I can see that now. The sparklies only covered the bad things in a thick covering of sweetness, but underneath, it was all still there.

Here, it's not like that at all. I'm at peace here, despite knowing what happened. Like I'm distant from my emotions.

For the first time in weeks, I can think rationally. Not the imposed cold rationality I gained by locking away my very essence. By holding everybody at arm's length.

"Can I have a moment?" I ask the Librarian and he gives me a nod. "Just call when you need me, or once you've made a decision."

As soon as he's out of sight, I run back to the centre of the room, where the large round table is sitting. I take one of the index cards and hastily scribble my mum's name on it, getting ink all over my fingers.

The card flashes and a moment later, a row of text appears below the name.

Spoke 19, 4th shelf on the right, third from the bottom.

I turn around in a circle, looking for the correct spoke. Luckily, each of the shelved corridors leading away from the centre space have metal signs strung above them.

I find number 19 and hasten along it until I'm standing in front of the fourth shelf. It's a more modern one than Mozart's book stood on, made of bright polished beechwood. I don't even have to look for the right book, it's glowing and vibrating as soon as I come close.

The book is a lot thinner than that of Mozart's, but it's lined with something that looks like burgundy silk, putting it apart from the other books on the shelf. Gingerly, I take it and open it at a random page.

There are no words in it, just sketches, in the style she used to plan her paintings. Delicate strokes, precise and purposeful. The first image I see is that of a baby with full cheeks and a large smile, lying on a large pillow. I assume that's me. It must have been shortly after I was brought to Earth and given to my parents.

I turn the page. Another picture of me, this time a little older, crawling on the floor, looking very pleased with myself. I smile at the same time as tears fill my eyes. Even though there are no words in my mother's book, I can feel her essence in it. The love she had for me. The love she had for living. She was always so full of energy and happiness.

I flick past more images of me as a child until I reach one of her and my dad. They're sitting on a bench, hand in hand, looking at each other with unmistakable love in their eyes. It doesn't show the setting of this memory, but it doesn't matter, the important thing is the feelings they had for each other. Even after so many years together, they could still have moments like that.

With a heavy feeling in my stomach, I turn to the final page. It's a sketch of a dark room; most of the paper is filled with rushed, thick pen strokes. In the darkness, a fuzzy shape of a man, looking straight at me. His eyes are as filled with love as the picture of the bench. My dad is showing her what she means to him. It must have been the last thing she saw before the Morrigan killed her. At least he was there with her. She wasn't completely alone.

I glide my fingers over the page. I almost expect the drawing to smudge, but it's somehow part of the page, the ink deep inside the paper. Suddenly desperate to see my mother's face one last time, I flick through the pages, but there are none. Sketches of her parents, of a young version of my dad, a lot of me, but not a single drawing of herself. As if she didn't think herself important enough to be in her very own book. She's always been far too modest. We had to persuade her to show her paintings in an exhibition, and even then, she didn't believe people would want to see them. Only when they were all bought within the first day at the gallery, she started to be a little more confident in her abilities. But even when she had dozens of orders, she still kept her modest, down-to-earth outlook on her art. She wasn't doing it for the money, but because she needed to let the paint out of her body, as she used to say. I never really understood that until I saw the book. Now I know what she meant.

Mum.

A tear drops on my father's face, and I know what to do. I need to go back, I need to find him and make sure he's safe. And I need to tell my Guardians that I want them to be look at me in the same way my dad looked at my mum, even after twenty years of marriage. I want them to be mine forever. I may not be worthy of them, but I'm going to try everything in my power to heal the gashes I drove between us in the past weeks.

I've been an idiot.

Beira might rule with coldness and little emotion, but I'm not Beira.

She's waning at the same time as the Summer King, Angus, is rising in power. She thinks I don't know, but I've noticed how her energy is less, how she looks a little lost sometimes.

She's getting weaker. Her method isn't working. I need passion to counter Angus and the Morrigan, not cold-hearted detachment from the world and those who love me.

And I certainly don't need sparklies. Maybe it's a good thing that Blaze is gone. Temptation can be an evil little thing, attacking you when you least expect it.

"Librarian?" I call out and carefully put my mother's book back in its place on the shelf.

"Yes, my dear?"

He's suddenly standing behind me, as if he appeared out of thin air. Somehow, that seems likely.

"I'd like to go back, please. I have a lot of unfinished business."

He smiles at me.

"Of course. Are there any other books you'd like to look at while you're here?"

I think about it for a moment. It would be tempting to see what my Guardians think about me. Or I could look at my father's book, but I'm scared to see what may be happening to him just now.

"Can you tell if a person is dead?"

He smiles again. "Your father is still alive, dear. But you already knew that, didn't you, in here..."

He points at his chest.

"Ready?"

I nod.

"Take me home."

Chapter Four

I'm not quite sure what happened. One second, I was in the Library, then standing back in my bathroom, lightning whipping all around me, then soft arms around my waist pulled me into darkness.

Now I'm kneeling on the snow-covered ground, my stomach heaving. Teleporting - or however you call what my mother just did - is not agreeing with me. The pool of vomit in front of me is proof of that.

I wipe my mouth and sit up, looking around. People are standing all over the place, talking in small groups, shooting me suspicious glances. We're in the Palace's main courtyard, so big that you can fit the weekly market in here and still have space. Ice sculptures line the paths, depicting a variety of animals. Most of them are ones you can find on Earth, but there are also unicorns, dragons and some I can't identify.

I struggle to my feet, swaying a little. I expended a lot of energy and feel like going back to bed. But first, I need to find my Guardians. I don't recognise most of the people around me. A few of them look vaguely familiar, probably guards or servants. My mother is nowhere to be seen. She must have dropped me here and then disappeared again. I try and convince myself that she had to rescue other people, but maybe she's mad at me. I would be. I'm furious at myself. I should have my magic under control by now.

I turn, looking in the direction of my sleeping quarters. They can't be seen from this part of the Palace, but there's a plume of smoke visible behind some of the turrets. I hope I didn't destroy too much. It was bad enough burning down half of my parents' home, but now, I seem to have progressed to palaces. Am I going to level cities next?

Just when I'd got used to my magic, it's beginning to scare me again. I feel for my heart cave. My magic is curled up, sleeping innocently as if nothing had happened. What a monster. Sometimes she's cute and does what I want, but it doesn't make up for the times she runs amok and almost kills people.

"Wyn!"

I whirl around, just in time to see Frost running towards me, before his arms pull me close and I don't see anything except for the dark blue shirt my face is smothered against. I breathe in deeply, relaxing when his sea breeze scent fills my lungs. It always reminds me of a walk on the beach on a stormy day.

"Wyn," he whispers, hiding his face in the remaining half of my hair. He presses me hard against his body, so much it almost hurts. His hands are running over my back, not gentle, but claiming, as if he's making sure I'm really there. That I'm still his.

"Frost," I say softly, wiggling a little to let him know that he's making it hard to breathe. As much as I like being hugged, crushing my ribcage isn't on my agenda.

"Give me a second to enjoy this," he sighs into my hair, "before you turn back into the Ice Princess."

Is that what he thinks of me? That I'm about to push him away?

Sadly, not long ago he would have been right. Before the Library I would have run away already, not even letting him hug me like this. But I've changed. At least I hope I have.

As much as I would like to give into the illusion that everything will suddenly be fine, I'm too rational for that. Grief and revenge are still fighting for dominance inside of me. I still don't think I can love my men the same way before the Morrigan killed my mother. There's too much darkness all around for that to happen.

Once she's defeated, I'll be able to move on, maybe.

No, I won't. I'll never forget how my mum was taken from me. How I was absolutely powerless, despite all the magic I possess.

Frost presses me even closer, now really threatening to crack my ribs.

"A... little... tight," I wince and he immediately lessens his hold on me.

"Sorry," he mutters, still refusing to let me go. "I wasn't sure if you'd make it out of there... And then when I saw Her Majesty's expression... I thought it was too late."

Finally, I notice that I'm not actually returning the hug. I'm too overwhelmed by his presence, by the memory of the Library still swirling in my mind.

I put my hands around his waist, touching the hard muscles on his back.

"I'm not planning to push you away," I whisper, only then noticing that he never said he'd expected me to do that. But it was probably obvious. I've done nothing else to the guys for days now.

"You're not?"

He grips my shoulders and - ironically - pushes me back, breaking the hug, until he can look at me. His blue eyes are swirling with emotion, the darkness of his irises overshadowing the slight green usually mixing with the blue.

"Do you really mean that?"

I nod, not quite trusting myself to speak. His expression is hard to read; I'm not sure if it's doubt or relief, or something else entirely.

"I need to hear that from you. I'm not sure I can believe it otherwise."

Something inside of me breaks. What did I do for my Guardian to say something like that?

Tears are flooding my eyes, tears I should have cried days ago.

"I won't push you away again," I repeat in a whisper. "And I'm sorry for what I did. I was a heartless bitch."

He chuckles softly. "I agree, but you had every reason to be."

I look over his shoulder, towards the plume of smoke still steadily climbing up into the sky.

"How bad is it?" I ask Frost and he pulls me closer again until my face is pressed against his chest, blocking the view of the destruction I wrought.

"Nobody got hurt. Your mother got them all out in time. I doubt that wing of the Palace will be liveable any time soon, though, unless her Majesty summons all the earth mages to make the repairs. There's only a handful here at the moment, the rest are spread all over the Realm."

"What about Crispin?"

The image of his crumpled, unconscious body flashes in my mind. The trickle of blood on his forehead.

He's alive, my bond is telling me that, and I'm sure Frost would have said something if it was serious.

"He'll be alright. He was awake last time I saw him, although he couldn't remember what happened. The healer is looking after him, don't worry."

I shake my head against his chest.

"Of course I worry. I could have killed him! I should never have lost control that way, I should know better by now. How can I be in charge of this Realm if I can't even protect my own men from myself?!"

I hate how whiny and insecure I sound, and I hate the tears soaking Frost's shirt even more. I need to be strong - not the ice cold Wyn I was until earlier today, but the normal me, the confident, steadfast Wyn. The Wyn who took on an entire demon army.

"Arc has a theory," Frost says slowly. "He thinks the unicorn's sparklies weakened your barriers, made it harder for you to control your magic. In the past few days, you've not used your powers much, and they've built up, pressing against your barriers like a dammed lake until the pressure got too much."

"Fucking sparklies," I grumble, cursing both the unicorn for giving them to me and myself for requesting them in the first place.

Frost laughs drily. "Yes, fucking sparklies. Once Blaze returns, I'm going to unscrew his horn so he'll never be able to give them to you again."

"Do you think he's gone for good?"

"I don't know. He's disappeared before, but usually he comes back when someone needs him. Well, us, really, I don't think he knows many Guardians. Or Princesses."

"How has he helped you?"

Frost grows silent and his breathing quickens slightly. I can hear his heart thump faster and immediately regret asking that question. I have no right to ask him personal questions after what I did. I need to rebuild some bridges first, I think. Figuring out how much damage I did to our relationship will take some time. Especially with Crispin. Gods, I almost killed him. I'd understand if he'll never forgive me for that. Although of course I want him to. He's mine, my Crispy, my Guardian.

The uncomfortable silence between us is broken by a shout.

"Princess!"

Frost lets go of me and I step back. Tamara is running towards us, her skirt bunched up in her hands so she can run faster.

She doesn't say anything until she's reached us, and even then, she only whispers.

"Her Majesty isn't well. You need to come, now."

My mother is lying on her bed, pale and frail looking. She's still in her clothes and boots, as if she didn't have the energy to climb under the covers.

It reminds me of the night when she was almost killed by an assassin using a Summer knife, forged by King Angus. He's the only one strong enough to kill her - or so I thought. Right now, she looks like she's severely ill. On death's door, almost.

"Mother?" I ask carefully, approaching her bed. She opens her eyes, but it seems she's having a hard time keeping them open. Her eyelids are fluttering and her pupils are dilated.

"Wyn," she rasps, her voice nothing like her usual strong, cold alto.

"What happened?" I address Tamara, not wanting my mum to speak.

"She expended too much energy rescuing everyone, and then breaking through the lightning storm to get you out as well." There's no accusation in Tamara's voice, just hard, honest fact. It hurts nonetheless.

"Has a healer been called?" I ask quietly, sitting down on the bed and gently taking my mother's hand. It's cold as always, but her grip is weak.

"There's nothing he can do. She needs time to get her strength back, but now that winter is almost over, it's getting harder for her to use her powers. It could be days, even weeks."

I squeeze my mum's hand tighter. I did this to her. She had to save these people because I put them in danger in the first place.

"Is there nothing I can do? I have magic, can I give her some of it? I'm her daughter, surely we're compatible?"

"This isn't like a blood transfusion," someone says and I whirl around, launching myself at Crispin, clutching him against my chest.

"You're okay!" I half-laugh, half-shout, my emotions all over the place. Then I remember that he might be hurt and quickly step back, checking for injuries. When I can't see any, I use my magic, scanning his body, but it seems that he's fully healed.

"I am," he says tonelessly, and my laughter dies off. He's angry at me. No, not angry, furious. His eyes are blazing, and I take a step back before I can stop myself.

His expression softens slightly before turning all business. He's the healer now, not my Guardian. Not the man I almost killed earlier.

"Your Majesty."

He approaches my mother's bed and takes the hand I was holding before he entered the room. Beira slowly opens her eyes, weakly looking around the room.

"Wyn," she whispers, almost inaudible.

"I'm here," I say quickly before she exhausts herself further, and step around the bed until I'm opposite Crispin.

He's hovering one hand over her stomach, his eyes closed. He must be feeling for injuries or weaknesses. I don't even need to use my own magic to know that my mother isn't injured as such. Her energy is gone almost entirely, and it seems that it has a much bigger effect on her than it would on anyone else. As a Goddess, maybe she's more reliant on magic? Does it keep her alive? Sustain her?

I put my hands on my mother's pale arm, visualising tendrils of magic running from mine into her body. Before I can even send them through her skin, something stops me. An obstacle, a barrier, preventing me from reaching her.

"I told you, it's not like a blood transfusion where you can simply send magic to someone," Crispin repeats, but a lot kinder this time. "It's possible to syphon magic in emergencies, like we did with you during your first flares, but you can't give someone else your own magic. They're incompatible, it would create chaos and even death. She'll have to recover on her own."

"He's right," Beira whispers. "You can't help me in that way, but I need your help for something else. I can't rule like this. I will be bed-bound for weeks."

I stifle a gasp. My mother is the strongest person, being, Goddess, whatever, that I know. She's been a little weaker recently, yes, but for her to stay in her bed for that long... it doesn't make sense. Is that what summer is doing to her?

"Is this normal?" I ask, feeling very naive.

"No," Crispin replies in my mother's stead. "She's always weaker during spring and summer, before getting stronger again in the autumn, but even in the middle of summer, she still has more magic than she seems to have just now."

He clears his throat and quickly adds, "Apologies, Your Majesty, for talking about you like that. You need to save your strength, so it's better if you don't talk too much."

I'm amazed at how brazen he is with Beira. As rebellious as my guys like to seem in private, they all have enormous respect for their Queen, and they usually talk to her with reverence. For Crispin to speak to her like that, he must really be worried that she might expend too much energy on talking with me.

"She used a massive amount of magic to keep the Palace from collapsing while she rescued the people in the wing you were in. Normally, she conserves her magic during spring so that she has some to draw from in the summer. Now, she's left with almost none, and with winter almost gone, it will take longer to regenerate."

The enormity of it all is making me woozy. With Beira this weak, the Realm is virtually defenceless. The Morrigan is meddling in the shadows, Angus is moving his troops for all to see, and demon sightings are becoming a normality. We need Beira to protect us. If we only had one enemy, we might succeed without her, but we have several, and all of them strong.

"Wyn."

I turn to my mother who's looking at me with an echo of her usual piercing glance, her eyes heavy-lidded.

"I need you to take over. I need you to rule."

Chapter Five

My guys are waiting outside for me and I fall into their arms, letting them comfort me by their simple touch.

Crispin is staying with my mother for now. It's probably better that way; I don't know what to say to him. Sorry for almost killing you? Sorry for crushing your skull? I don't think that sounds very good.

Arc is hugging me tight, pressing me against his chest, while the other two are holding me from behind. I'm surrounded by them, and I'm tempted to just let myself go, let my feelings take over and have them hold me together. But I can't. My mother told me to rule. I'm the Princess and for once, I need to behave like it.

Still, I enjoy my men's touch and I don't push them away. On the contrary, I melt into Arc's embrace, snuggling against the soft fabric of his shirt, feeling the hard muscles underneath. I can't resist, I pull his shirt out of his kilt and slide my hands underneath, touching his bare back.

He grumbles softly, his chest vibrating against mine. I feel my nipples harden at the sensation. This really isn't the place, but I can't stop.

I lift my head and see that Arc has been waiting for me. His lips crash on mine. He doesn't even wait for me to open my mouth, already his tongue is pressing against my lips, ready to enter my mouth.

I squeeze his hips, pulling him closer, his crotch pressing against my stomach. He's getting hard, just like I am feeling tingles spread between my legs.

"Let's find ourselves a room," Frost suggests with a chuckle. I love how he automatically assumes that all three of us are going to be together. Maybe Crispin, if he wants to join us, but somehow, I doubt that.

With a pang of regret, I break the kiss, but Arc growls when I do.

"Dinnae stop," he mutters and lifts me into his arms at the same time as his lips meet mine again. I smile and return the kiss, my heart beating faster at the thought of what's about to happen.

This is the first time I'm kissing one of them since my mum died. Should I really be doing this? My mum is dead and my other one is lying in the room next door, too weak to even sit up.

But then I decide that yes, I should be doing this. I have a bond to reforge. Four bonds, in fact. I need my men for the days and weeks to come, and not just that. I need to feel alive again.

Arc carries me somewhere, but I have my eyes closed, all my senses tuned into our kiss. It's magical. Our tongues are dancing while at the same time, his hands are gripping my arse, kneading it while holding me in his arms.

"My turn."

A gruff voice breaks through the passionate bliss filling my mind, and with one last nip at his bottom lip, I break the kiss and turn my head towards Storm. We seem to have entered a room, but I couldn't care less where we are. Without warning, Storm's lips are on mine, continuing what Arc started.

Hands grip my hips and I'm lifted from Arc's arms, but I'm too busy exploring Storm's mouth to protest.

I'm put back on my feet, and this time, I'm about to complain, already missing the warmth of my Guardian's embrace, but then someone is sliding his hands under my shirt, reaching around until they're on my stomach. The scent of a sea breeze fills me nostrils before Frost's lips touch the back of my neck.

He presses tiny kisses on my skin and goosebumps run down my spine and straight into my core. At the same time, Arc is fumbling with my pyjama bottoms, trying to open the knot in the cord holding them up. I hadn't even realised I was still in my bedclothes, but of course, I've not had any chance to change since I woke up. I don't think I'm wearing underwear, either. I blush at the thought of them undressing me after they brought me back from Blaze's cave. Such a pity I was unconscious. Although I wouldn't have appreciated their attention at the time. But I do now.

Arc's become too impatient and a moment later, rips my pyjamas apart. Silly Guardian. Hot Guardian. My torn trousers sink to the floor, pooling around my ankles. Then his mouth is on my right arse cheek, nibbling on my sensitive skin, and I moan against Storm's mouth.

All of them are kissing me at the same time and it's almost too much to bear.

Arc hugs my thighs from both sides, pulling my hips back so he has better access to my naked arse. Frost is gliding his hands upwards, leaving my belly and reaching the very edges of my breasts. He's slow, far too slow, and I moan again, wanting his hands on my boobs.

"Who are you moaning for, Princess?" Frost asks seductively, running a finger over the skin just beneath my left breast. Tingles are spreading all over my body and my legs are beginning to shake. Every single one of my four Guardians is intense, and together, they're incredible. Overwhelming. Amazing.

Finally, Frost takes my left nipple between his thumb and index finger and squeezes it gently.

"Do you like that?"

What an idiot! Who wouldn't?

Arc chooses that moment to slide a finger into me from below and this time, my legs really buckle. If Storm wasn't holding me, I would have collapsed to the floor in a heap of pleasure.

"Or do you prefer what Arc's doing?" Frost is teasing me, but Storm's kiss is preventing me from answering. My hard nipples and moans should be enough of an answer, though.

Storm growls, apparently not happy that he's not been mentioned yet. Frost chuckles and takes my other nipple between my fingers, squeezing harder this time.

"Or is it Storm who's making you moan?"

Ironically, Storm breaks the kiss right then, leaving me panting. My lips are swollen and tingly all over, desperate for even more attention from the guys. So is the rest of my body. I need them all, their touch, everywhere.

"I am," Storm says in a voice that allows no protest. He lifts me up, removing me from the other two. I'm about to protest, but stop when he lies me down on a bed - we seem to be in one of the guest rooms - and pulls off his jeans. I lift my head to watch as he slides down his boxers, revealing his hard cock. If I thought I was wet before then, I really am now.

I spread my legs, ready to take him in.

"Why is my brother always the first?" Frost complains jokingly, but he's too late. Surprisingly slowly, Storm presses against my entrance, giving me a moment to prepare, before he gently slides in. I should be used to his size by now, but every time, I feel like I'm tight as a virgin when I take him. He gives me the time to adjust, looking down at me with eyes filled with love and desire. I never thought I'd have one man look at me like that, but now I have four.

Arc is sitting down on the bed from the other side, also naked, also very, very ready for me. I stretch out a hand, gripping his cock. He groans and adjusts his position so it's more comfortable for both of us. Frost kneels next to my hips, his knees touching my skin. Even this simple, accidental touch makes my skin burst into flames. He's supposed to be the water Guardian, but his touch is full of heat.

He leans forward and takes my right nipple into his mouth, sucking hard. I gasp as pain mixes with pleasure, and he takes it as encouragement to do it again. With one hand, he massages my breast while the other has somehow made its way down and is gently rubbing my bud, sending tiny shockwaves deep inside, making my inner walls contract around Storm.

His thrusts are getting harder now that he's made sure that I can take it. Every time he slams into me, I slide my hand along Arc's cock, his groans mixing with mine.

Storm grips my thighs and pulls them up, widening his access. His eyes are half closed and he's breathing heavily, just like me, just like the others. All of us are united in the pleasure that's lifting us away from reality and into a state of blissful separation from our duties and worries.

"What are you doing to me!" Storm suddenly shouts and I look at him in shock, wondering if I did something wrong. But he's smiling at me when he sees my confusion. "I used to think I had stamina, but you... I can't hold out much longer."

"Then let go," I whisper hoarsely. "Don't hold back."

He looks deep into my eyes, his pupils shrunk to pinpricks surrounded by fire. Then he nods, as if he's giving permission both to himself and to me, and plunges back into me with one hard thrust, making me arch my back and grip Arc's cock tightly.

My other hand is suddenly gripped by Frost's and he holds me tight as his brother fucks me. Storm really is letting go of all restraints, gripping my thighs so tightly it hurts. But it's a good pain. One that I welcome as it mixes with the sensations of all three Guardians loving my body. Loving me.

With one final thrust, Storm comes in me, making my inner walls shudder and contract hard against his cock. He releases my legs but stays inside me, quivering. He's looking at me with a strange expression, but before I can think any more about it, he leans forward and pulls me up, his lips meeting mine. His taste is salty from the tiny beads of sweat that have collected above his upper lip. Somehow, that makes it even better.

I kiss him hard, wrapping my arms around him, holding him close.

"I wasn't sure if... " he whispers when he breaks the kiss. He docsn't continue, but I can guess what he means. I pushed them away, and they must have had doubts that I'd let them in again. Time to prove that particular side of me is gone and banished.

"Kiss me," I ask. No, it's more of a demand. He gives me a surprised look but does as I said. I let my tongue slip into his mouth, gliding along his teeth before intensifying the kiss, staking my claim on him. I put all the love I feel for him into that kiss, showing him exactly how much he means to me. How much they all mean to me. I'm not going to let them go.

Arc groans and I notice I still have my hand wrapped around his cock, but I've stopped stroking him. I playfully nudge Storm's tongue one last time, before breaking the kiss and letting myself fall back onto the mattress.

"I think Arc needs some relief," I chuckle and Storm steps back, leaving me feeling empty.

But not for long. Quicker than I can see, Arc has moved around the bed and has taken Storm's place between my legs. This time, it's easy to take him, now that the other Guardian has already stretched me inside.

Still, I can't stop a moan escaping my lips as Arc fills me completely, reaching even further than Storm did. Frost's mouth is back on my nipples, but this time, I nudge his hips until he gives me access to his cock, expecting to feel cloth but instead get smooth, velvety skin. When did he change? Has he been naked the entire time?

I gently begin to stroke him, doing the same to Frost as I did to Arc. I lift my head to see Storm watching us with a satisfied smile. It seems like he's hard again already. Well, there are two other men to satisfy first. Then we can start at the beginning again.

Arc is pumping into me, his face and chest flushed. Together with his red hair, he looks adorable. If only he was still wearing his kilt. One day, I need to ask him to do that. I want the whole sexy Scotsman experience.

But for now, I'm happy with the way he moves in me, the sounds he makes, the euphoria he brings me. When he comes, I do too, contracting around him, making our connection even more intense. While I'm still in the rush of the climax, Frost takes Arc's place, starting slowly, moving in and out at a steady pace.

Arc lies down beside me and his lips meet mine, hungrily kissing me while his hands are playing with my breasts.

Storm joins us on my other side.

"Never leave us again," he whispers when his brother does his last hard thrusts and my body begins to shake in yet another orgasm. "You don't know what it does to us when you're not around."

I nod, breaking the kiss with Arc. He groans in disappointment but I ignore him for the moment.

"Never again," I promise. "I'm yours."

Chapter Six

Reality hits me far too quickly. I managed to sleep for a few hours after exhausting myself with my men, but as soon as I wake up, I know it's time to take on my responsibility.

Just before I drifted off to sleep, Tamara came in, letting me know that there had been no change in my mother's condition. I felt guilty for not sitting by her bedside, but what good would that do. It was far more important to reinstate the bonds with my Guardians, whose help I'll need now more than ever before.

I'm to rule. I have no idea how to do that. I've tried learning more about the Realm, about how my mother keeps everything going, and how she deals with her Council. I've been to most Council sessions, so that will definitely help. I know them all, and I know some of their weaknesses and strengths. I'm sure there will be members of the Council who will not approve of me taking over while Beira is sick.

Theodore, the physician, and Magnus, the treasurer, aren't my biggest fans. They probably see me as a threat to their own power. Luckily, Tamara, Gwain and Ada are all on my side. I'm not quite sure about Algonquin and Zephyr, but I know that if I get one of them to support me, the other will follow.

In the end, they will all have to follow my mother's wishes, but it's on them to decide whether they'll make it easy or hard for themselves. We're at war and there's no time for infighting. I hope these men aren't too stuck in their traditions to realise that.

"Ready for today?" Frost asks me softly, noticing that I'm awake. I'm sandwiched between him and his brother, with Arc's arm flung across Storm so he can have his hand on my hip. When I concentrate on it, I can feel a trickle of energy flow between the four of us. Our bond.

I don't know where Crispin is. Maybe still with my mother. He didn't join us last night, even though the bed would have been large enough to accommodate him as well. It's in his right to be angry with me though. There's no excuse for what I did. I should have kept control, even with the unicorn sparklies clouding my mind.

Frost pulls me closer and I remember that he asked me a question.

"I wouldn't call it ready. I don't think I'm prepared for this, but I'll do what's required of me and will try and fill my mother's role as well as I can."

"Spoken like a true Princess." He smiles and gives me a quick kiss on the cheek. "Storm will be with you in the Council. You won't be alone."

"What about the rest of you?"

He chuckles. "We'll be busy preparing for war."

Before I leave the room, I wrap a colourful scarf around my head to hide my bald patch. I need to find a better solution for this soon, but I don't have the time right now. A scarf will have to do. And unsurprisingly, my new Demigoddess beauty is making me look good even with this on my head.

When I arrive at the Council Chamber, Gwain is waiting for me outside. The Master of Arms is looking distraught, a look I've not seen on him before.

"Your Highness... a word?"

I nod and he leads me along a corridor, away from the Council. When we're out of earshot from any curious noble, he stops and looks at me with a pained expression.

"Ada has disappeared."

"What?"

Ada is his second in command, a woman with her own harem of Guardians. The last time I'd seen her had been with the dragon prisoner in the dungeons. She'd been in charge of interrogating him, although even she hadn't managed to get much out of the dragon shifter."

"She left last night. There's a note..."

I frown in irritation.

"Last night? Why am I only hearing about this now?"

He shifts uncomfortably on his feet. "Tamara told me to wait until today to tell you, she said you were busy."

Now it's my turn to look uncomfortable. I was busy indeed, exploring my Guardians' bodies inside out. Still, I would have made myself available for something as important as this.

"What's on the note?" I ask brusquely and he takes a folded piece of paper from his waistcoat pocket.

I stretch out my hand to take it but instead, he unfolds it.

"It's written in code, Your Highness. Even knowing the cypher, I can't make much sense out of it though. She says she needs to leave, that she has to do something that will aid the war effort. She doesn't say what. There's several sentences in which she apologises, and that she hopes we won't treat her as a traitor."

"Why would we do that? A deserter, perhaps, but a traitor?"

Gwain clears his throat. "Ada isn't the only one who's gone. She took the prisoner with her. The dragon."

Anger fills me. "And you didn't think to tell me?"

I had hoped that the Master of Arms would support me, see me as a worthy heir. Instead, he didn't even bother to inform me that a prisoner escaped.

"We didn't make the connection until about an hour ago when the guards told me that the dragon was gone." He pauses, then looks at me gravely. "I'm wondering if he managed to bewitch her somehow. Manipulate her. We know almost nothing about the powers dragons possess, and it could well be within the realms of the possible that he made her leave."

He's right. When the prisoner was caught, Algonquin provided us with all the books on dragons from the Royal

Library. There weren't many and most of them were based on legends or hearsay, not on actual facts.

"What about her men?" I ask.

"Gone."

"Then I doubt that she was manipulated to leave. She would have needed some excellent arguments for them to come with her. The dragon convincing her, maybe, but also the three men? No, I think she must have a genuine reason."

I sigh. "Are we going to search for her?"

"Usually I'd say yes, but at the moment, our soldiers are needed more urgently here and in our outposts." He clears his throat again. "I propose that Storm takes her place. I know he is head of your personal guard, but you have three others to keep you safe. We need his expertise and authority."

To be honest, I had already planned to give Storm a more important role on the Council. This might actually turn out to be quite convenient. Not that it doesn't upset me that Ada left. We'd had a few chats about being in a relationship with several men at once, and had begun to form the beginnings of a friendship.

A gong sounds through the corridor, the signal that the Council session is about to begin.

"Anything else?" I ask Gwain, mentally preparing for yet more bad news.

"No, nothing that needs your attention personally."

"Good, then let's get this over with."

I turn and stride along the hallway, leaving him behind. I feel like a real Princess, suddenly, strong and confident and a tiny bit ruthless.

Everyone but Theodore is in attendance. He's looking after my mother so that Crispin can get some rest. I make a mental note to seek out my healer Guardian after this meeting, to check if he's alright. It must have been exhausting to stay with Beira all night. Maybe it's made him even more resentful towards me. I sigh inwardly. Even more issues to fix. How did I manage to break so many things during one week of grief and madness?

Instead of my usual place on my mother's side, this time, I take the seat at the head of the table, the chair that looks almost like a throne. It's surprisingly uncomfortable. No wonder my mother always keeps these sessions as brief as possible.

"You'll all know by now that my mother won't be able to attend the Council meetings for a while," I begin. "She's asked me to take her place until she's recovered."

I watch their reactions. Tamara is smiling at me reassuringly, as is Storm. There's pride in his eyes, and it makes my stomach do little flips of happiness. I made him sit in Ada's usual place, so that it's immediately clear to all that he's taking over her role.

There's been no protest about that. They all know he's the right person for the job. He's been ready for more responsibility for a long time.

The problem with Guardians is that they live forever. They don't usually retire, so to move up in the hierarchy, Guardians have to hope that their superior moves, disappears or dies. No wonder there's so much intrigue in this place.

Zephyr is smiling at me as well. That's a good sign. The Master of the Wings is a hard man to read; I'm never quite sure if his confused appearance is real or fake.

The librarian, Algonquin, is looking at me with a blank expression. Time will tell if he'll support me or not.

However, I'd much rather take his blankness than the outrage Magnus is openly showing. What was he expecting to happen? For him to take my mother's place? Or for the Council to take over and rule together, rather than be the supporting advisors?

As much as I support democracy on Earth, for the Realm, it doesn't make as much sense. Beira is a Goddess, the Mother of Gods. Even if she wasn't ruling, people would still turn to her for help. She'd never be able to not play an important role – or *the* most important role.

She's a Queen through and through, and that won't change. I can't wait for her to be back on her feet.

I turn to the Mistress of the Household. "Tamara, I believe you have an update on my mother's health?"

She nods. "She's stable and was talking a little this morning. She repeated her wish that Princess Wynter acts as her replacement."

I smile at her, grateful for the reassertion. The more often Magnus and Theodore hear this, the more likely it is that they'll support me eventually. Pity the healer isn't here. Maybe I should ask Tamara to spread the message throughout the Palace, so that everybody knows what's happening. It will need some thinking about. I don't want my mother to appear weak, but at the same time, I can't afford for people to think that I don't have the authority to enforce whatever I need to do to win this war.

"Good. You will have noticed that Storm is sitting in Ada's place. Ada has left on an important mission and will likely not be back for some time. Therefore, Gwain and I have decided to promote Storm to Deputy Master in Arms, reporting directly to Gwain and myself. One of my other three Guardians will take over his role as the head of my personal guard, so don't worry, I won't be left defenceless."

I smile drily. I don't think most of them are aware that Storm isn't actually the leader of the four. They're all equal, and they let him pretend to be the head of my guard when it's needed. He is the most dominant of the four, so the role fits him.

"Now, I believe Gwain has some more to update us on."

The Master of Arms stands and gives me a small bow.

"Yes, Your Highness. There have been attacks on the Southern Gate. We managed to defeat the Summer soldiers, but we took heavy losses. I've dispatched reinforcements and additional healers to all the Gates. We need to prepare however that eventually, they will manage to break through. I don't know if you're aware, but two decades ago, Angus managed to get some of his warriors into the Realm without the use of the Gates. In response, Queen Beira strengthened the invisible defences of the Realm, but we don't know how long they will hold. Especially now..."

I swallow hard. I know that story. Those were the Summer soldiers who killed my father. Yet another reason to hate Angus.

"If he attacks and breaks through one of the Gates, how quickly will we get the rest of the army there?" I ask and am surprised when Gwain averts his eyes.

"Usually, Queen Beira would transport a large number of them, giving the rest time to fly there themselves. But now... we'll have to spread out our forces across the Realm, making it easier for them to congregate in one place should the need arise."

"When the need arises," Tamara corrects. "There's no question that we'll be attacked soon. Who knows whether it will be Angus first or the Morrigan, or maybe they're working together and will combine their forces." She looks straight at me. "Princess, I think you should have a talk with your mother and see if you may perhaps have inherited the power of transporting others across distances. Other Gods can teleport themselves, and maybe one or two others, but Queen Beira is the only one besides Angus who can take large amounts of people with them. If you had the same power, well, we'd have an additional way of fighting them."

"I will speak to her later today," I promise. I was planning to talk to her about my new lightning powers anyway. I've never heard of anyone having lightning magic before, but maybe I've just not talked to the right people. It was a shock to have yet another new magic. Maybe it was the sparklies that caused it. Maybe it wasn't real lightning after all, just a side effect of all the unicorn magic I'd absorbed. Whatever it was, it had been incredibly powerful and explosive. If I could harness that power, it would be a powerful weapon against our enemies.

I cringe. Here I am, talking about enemies and war and death. Not long ago, I was an almost-human on Earth, having romantic notions about living in the Realm as a Princess. I never imagined there'd be war. I didn't think anyone would dare stand against my mother.

And now, we don't have just one enemy, but several. If what Chesca said is true, the Morrigan is controlling the demons that are attacking our borders almost daily now. Then there's Angus and his twisted hate for Beira. Bad enough to have one, but we have two, one as powerful as the other. Angus may have the better warriors, but the Morrigan has a mind more cruel and evil than I can even imagine. I shudder when I think of what she did to Crispin. How she manipulated him into hurting and killing others.

"Tamara, any news on the Morrigan? Did the man who brought us the message give us any leads?"

'Message' sounds a lot better than 'the chest that contained my dead mother's hand'. The messenger took poison when he arrived, dying almost instantly.

"We retraced his steps for a bit but then his tracks disappeared. He came from the North, and he was on foot, he didn't fly."

I frown. "So he wasn't a Guardian?"

"He was. He'd had his wings removed."

A collective gasp echoes through the room. I didn't even know that was possible. Our wings aren't like you imagine angels' wings, always visible, always connected to our bodies. They only pop into existence when we call for them, and even then, they're ethereal, not quite as solid as they should be considering that they carry us through the air. I've got enough practice now that if someone gripped one of my wings, I could make them disappear before they could hurt me. So how did the Morrigan cut off this man's wings?

There's no doubt that it was her. It's such a twisted thing to do, something so evil and cruel that I can't imagine Angus being responsible for it. He's a brute and he's single-minded about what he wants. He's out in the open and makes up his lack of subterfuge in numbers and his warriors' skills.

I decide not to ask about the details of how the man was tortured before he brought us the message.

"Any idea where he might have come from? What's in the North?"

Algonquin gets up and takes a rolled-up map from a shelf behind him, before spreading it out on the table in the centre of the room.

The Palace and the surrounding towns are in the centre of the Realm, slightly more West than East. I recognise some of the names of smaller towns and villages from previous Council meetings. Most of the inhabited areas are in the Southern half of the Realm, with only small dots showing that people are living in dwellings further North.

Algonquin points to a strange runic symbol on the top of the map, straight at the Northern edge of the Realm.

"There's a ruined Gate up there, but it's been broken for centuries, millennia even. I believe it's checked on every year or so, but maybe someone should take a closer look, just in case."

"How does a Gate break?" I ask in confusion. I thought they were unbreakable, eternal gateways between the Realms.

Algonquin gives me a strange look. "By a demigod travelling through it while having a magic flare. The Gate exploded, and so did the demigod."

I shudder. "Who was it?"

"You wouldn't have heard of him. He died on the day he came of age, when his powers erupted. He'd been in the Realms to visit his parents, and everybody thought that his magic would develop the next day, but they got it wrong. His raw, untamed power tore the Gate apart."

I swallow past the stone that seems to have lodged itself in my throat. I travelled through a Gate in the days after my own magic had flared up several times. Had I been in danger? Could I have destroyed the Gate we used?

I shrug off these uncomfortable thoughts. "Okay, check on the Gate. If it's working again and letting people into the Realm, we need to know about it."

"Yes, Your Majesty," Algonquin says with a bow, before his expression changes in embarrassment as everyone in the room suddenly seems busy clearing their throats.

It seems like the librarian is on my side after all.

Chapter Seven

After the Council session, I feel both depleted and restless. My advisors had painted a much bleaker picture of the situation than I expected. People are dying while trying to keep the Realm safe. There are invaders at our doorstep and we won't be able to keep them out for much longer. How does my mother cope with this kind of pressure?

Well, maybe I'll get to ask her in a moment. I'm headed towards her chambers, Arc in tow. Storm had to stay to talk to Gwain, making plans for his promotion. Usually, there'd be a big ceremony, but half of the army is stationed away from the Palace just now, and there's not really the mood for a celebration either. Knowing Storm, he'll try to wiggle out of any kind of formal affair.

"How are ye feeling?" Arc asks me.

"Like I either want to fly away and murder two Gods, or like hiding under my blanket with my Guardians by my side, hoping that it'll all be over soon." I sigh. "Please stop me from doing either."

He laughs. "I wouldnae stop ya from jumping into bed with me. But we wouldnae be hiding in there..."

I can't help but smile. That's my Arc, the funny, kilted Scot who's wormed his way into my heart with his hilarious accent and attitude. I'm so thankful I have him and the others. I really would be hiding otherwise, pretending that this responsibility of ruling a Realm didn't exist.

"Want me ta come in with ya?" he asks when we reach the door to my mother's bedchamber. There are four guards posted outside, twice the normal number. I keep having to remind myself that she's not as invincible as she usually is. If someone attacked her now, she wouldn't be able to do much to stop them.

"No, it's alright. Although if Theodore is in there, maybe call him out with some sort of distraction? I want to talk to my mother alone."

He grimaces at my mention of the healer. Seems I'm not the only one finding him annoying.

"Aye, I'll come up with an excuse."

I take his hand and give it a squeeze, both as a thank you to him and reassurance for me.

My mother's room is dimly lit by a few of the glowing magic orbs that are used instead of lightbulbs in the Palace. The curtains are drawn closed, shutting out the cold midday sun.

I send a little magic to the closest orb until it starts to glow brighter.

Beira is lying in her bed, sleeping peacefully. Her skin is pale though, and her breath is clearly audible in the quiet room. There is no sign of Theodore; he must have left shortly before I arrived. Maybe he's gone to tell Crispin to take over again. As much as I want to speak to my healer Guardian, I'd prefer if he didn't come just now. I need some time alone with my mother.

"Mum?" I ask quietly, and her eyes flutter open immediately.

"Wyn. Come closer," she says in a raspy whisper. There's a glass of water on the small bedside drawer and I take it with me as I approach her. I help her sit up a little so she can drink. It's scary how easy it is for me to lift her. She's so light, so frail. How did my mother change from an almighty Goddess into this sickly woman?

Oh yes, it's all my fault. I'd tried to forget that fact.

"Thank you." Her voice is a lot smoother now that she's had some water. She leans back against the pillow I fluffed up for her and looks at me with an echo of her usual piercing eyes.

"How was the meeting?"

I sigh a little. "Bleak. Ada has run away, Storm has taken her place, Algonquin thinks that the Northern Gate may have been used by the Morrigan's messenger, and the Southern Gate has been attacked repeatedly. For now, it seems all we can do is wait for our scouts and spies to bring us more information."

"You sound as if you've already got a good understanding of the situation. I'd hoped to spare you from taking over more duties for a while, but it wasn't to be."

She coughs and I hand her the glass of water again.

"There's something Tamara said," I begin, watching her drink in small sips. "She was wondering whether I can do the same teleportation magic you do, to transport our soldiers to where they're needed."

My mother frowns, thinking for a moment before she answers. "It's not like normal magic. It's more like wings, something we're born with and while it needs a bit of practice, we instinctively know how to do. You've never accidentally teleported somewhere, have you?"

I shake my head.

"Then it's unlikely that you possess that skill. It's something only Gods can do, I'm sorry." She smiles at my disappointed look. "But you have some other magic we should talk about. Was that the first time you used lightning?"

"Yes. It just came out of nowhere, I've never felt anything like it before. It was very... overwhelming. Violent. Hard to control."

"I could see that," she says drily and I cringe when I think of what my magic cost her. "Don't feel bad. Nobody knew that you were going to be in danger of having another flare, myself included, or I would have done something about it. What's happening to me is natural. Spring is coming, Winter is disappearing. It's why Angus has been waiting until now to make his big moves. Luckily, we have you."

"I'm not much use, I still can't even control my magic. How am I supposed to make other people do what I say if they know how unpredictable I am? None of the people who were in the collapsed Palace wing will ever trust me again - I almost killed them! If you hadn't been there, they'd all be buried beneath tons of stone."

I fight against the urge to punch something. The wall, or maybe myself. I'd punch my magic if she wasn't holed up in her cave, purring innocently. I'm going to need to have a serious talk with her. She doesn't care at all about what's happening to the real world as the effect of her power tantrums.

"They don't know it was you," my mother whispers, her voice slowly getting weaker again. "And even so, you're my daughter. They will accept you. Now, go to the library and seek out Algonquin. Have him give you anything he has about lightning magic. But before, tell Tamara to contact Thor. I think he may be the perfect teacher for you."

Thor doesn't quite look like he does in the films, but that's not a bad thing. Not at all. If I didn't already have my four Guardians... well, let's just say I have a hard time not drooling. That may be due to the lack of his shirt. Yes, he's showing off his bare chest, wearing nothing but loose leather trousers and black boots. And his hammer, of course, in a sheath around his waist. Tiny lightning bolts are sizzling around it, looking very much like the magic I produced yesterday.

"So, you're Beira's little spawn?" he asks me in a deep voice as I approach him in my mother's vestibule. Other nobles and a few minor Gods are standing on both sides of the room, watching us curiously. I'm sure everybody in the Palace is about to know that Thor called me a 'spawn'.

"Her daughter, actually. And you, are you one of her creations?" I shoot back and watch gleefully as he raises his bushy eyebrows in surprise.

"I am, actually. Does that make us siblings?" He howls in laughter at the disgusted expression I'm sure my face is showing.

"No. Cousins, maybe? Twice-removed, at least?" I add that so I don't feel bad about ogling his stunning physique. I don't want to look at my brother/cousin/whatever that way. The whole concept of my mother creating other Gods is still a bit too much to grasp. She also made my father, so maybe Thor is my uncle? Urgh, Wyn, stop that train of thought. There's no genetic similarity between me and Thor.

"I like you, Godspawn. Well met."

He stretches out a hand and I take it, squeezing hard to show that I'm not intimidated by him - even though his hand is almost twice as large as mine.

"Nice to meet you." I was tempted to reply with 'well met' as well, but that was a bit too medieval for me. He's allowed to speak like someone from a film, but not me. I'm your standard down-to-earth Demigoddess.

I notice how the room has become very quiet. All eyes are on us. I feel a little uncomfortable, very aware of the scarf I have wrapped around my head. They must all be wondering why I'm wearing it.

"Let's go somewhere a little more private," I suggest and he grins at me.

"Are you propositioning me?"

"I certainly am not. I just don't want the ladies of the Court to faint." I nod towards one female Guardian to my right, who's obviously overwhelmed by staring at Thor's muscled body. She's fanning herself and blushes when she notices us looking at her.

"You're right. My wife wouldn't be happy about that."

That makes me stop in my tracks. "You're married?!"

Oh, poor women of this world. Yet another good-looking man who's no longer available.

"Of course, didn't you know that? Sif likes to stay at home though, making sure our daughter doesn't get into too much trouble."

"Wait, you have a daughter?"

"Didn't they teach you anything?" he grumbles as if offended by my ignorance.

"But I was told that Gods can't have children... it's not allowed."

"Which is why we adopted Pippa. She was born on Earth but grew up in my Realm. I've been trying to make her go and explore Earth so she can see where she came from, but so far, she's refused. Maybe I should get her to talk to you. You can have a bit of girl talk."

A bit of... Who does he think I am?!

I'm a little bit busy fighting a war at the moment, I don't have time to tell a girl to spread her wings and leave her parents' nest. Although I suppose that if she's human, she doesn't have wings. Look at me, already used to the idea of everybody in the Realms having wings. I'm adapting quickly... kind of.

I decide not to say anything and simply motion him to follow me out of the vestibule and through several corridors until we've reached one of the training courtyards. Storm's reserved this one for me, so we should be undisturbed here.

I try and ignore all the stares people are giving us on our way there, and sigh in relief when the doors close behind us and we step into the fresh, cool air outside.

Thor unbuckles his belt and I'm about to protest, thinking he's got some kind of exhibitionism planned, when I see that he's simply removing the sheath his hammer is in. He puts it on the ground and stretches his legs.

"It gets a bit heavy, sometimes," he admits. "But people want to see the hammer so I'll have to take it wherever I go."

No, I did not expect him to say that. Maybe some comment about how big his hammer is, how hard, that kind of thing. Instead, he sounds almost annoyed at how people are worshipping him.

"Do you need the hammer to do magic?" I ask, genuinely interested.

"No, although it helps direct the energy more efficiently. Lightning is a volatile force, and it's easier to control if there's a conductor. I could use a rod or something like that, but Beira decided to give me a hammer so now I'm stuck with that."

"My mum gave you that hammer?"

"Do you ask a lot of questions?" he retorts and I give him a disapproving frown - which he doesn't care about in the least.

"As much as I would like to answer all your questions, my wife expects me to be back for dinner, so let's start with your training. I'm told you can summon lightning - mind giving me a demonstration?"

I shrug. "Sure, but last time, I levelled an entire part of the Palace, so you may want to step back."

His eyes widen slightly before he smooths his expression into something between boredom and curiosity. What a strange man... God. Are all of the major Gods this intense? This arrogant?

Luckily, he follows my advice and retreats to one side of the courtyard while I take up position in the centre. I'm not quite sure what I'm doing; after all, last time I created lightning was a complete accident. I remember it started with little sparks around my hands. Maybe if I can reproduce those, I can summon proper lightning after.

I concentrate on my magic, coaxing her out of her cave. She stretches and yawns, but then jumps towards me, happy to be let free. I tell her that I need lightning, but she just rubs against my legs and purrs. Thanks, that's not very helpful.

With the other elements, I can usually draw from them in the environment. Water and air are the easiest, fire the hardest. But lightning... where am I supposed to get that from?

I look up at the sky. Not a cloud in sight, and especially no storm clouds.

I sigh. "I don't know how to begin," I admit.

Thor smirks. "Lightning for beginners, I get it. First of all, what is lightning?"

"Ehm... big lightning bolts coming down from the sky during thunderstorms?" Even I know how silly that sounds. "Electricity?" I add, hoping that one will be less stupid.

Thor shakes his head in frustration. "What do they teach you on Earth? Lightning is an electrostatic discharge. Imagine two electrically charged objects, like balloons you've rubbed against a woollen tunic. If you make them touch each other, electricity will flow between them for just a moment. When it's just a small electric charge, sparks will fly. If it's larger, much larger, you get lightning."

So far, I'm following, even though physics was never my strongest subject. "But where do I get electrically charged objects from? Do I need to bring balloons onto the battlefield?"

I chuckle at my own joke and even Thor can't hide a grin.

"No, Godspawn, all you need can be found around you."

I have a lightbulb moment. "You mean protons and electrons and that kind of stuff?"

He sighs indulgently. "Yes, that kind of stuff. But if it helps you, just imagine the air around you sizzle with energy. Imagine how there are millions of particles, ready to be pushed together to produce lightning. When you picture it correctly in your mind, the magic will follow."

Okay then. That shouldn't be too hard. I focus again and imagine everything around me sparkling with energy. It's not the first time that I'm glad I have such an active imagination. Years of cultivating my imaginary friends is now paying off.

When I have the air saturated with sparks of electricity, I draw some magic into me and spread it through the space in front of me, until it touches the sparks.

With a deep breath, I pull on the magic, forcing the sparks to touch each other.

A lightning bolt rams into the ground in front of me, barely missing my feet. I jump back in surprise, but stumble and manage to fall flat on my arse. Ouch. Has the ground always been that hard? This is going to leave a bruise. Maybe I can get Crispin - no, I can't.

Thor is laughing wildly and I scramble to my feet, glaring at him.

"Was your first attempt that much better?" I ask him, barely hiding a growl.

"Of course it was. I'm the God of Thunder, making lightning bolts is what I do."

He's got a point. At least I know that I have other magic he doesn't have. My mother explained to me that the major Gods all have one or two main powers, and the minor Gods only one. Usually, they all have basic capabilities in other elemental magic, but I'd definitely outrank them in having several major powers. Probably not as strong as theirs, but at least I have strength in numbers.

"Try again," Thor tells me and steps back again, this time a little further than before. Is he worried I might accidentally hit him?

He's probably right. Just now, I'd unsuccessfully aimed for the lightning bolt to hit the other end of the courtyard. Certainly not in front of my feet. I'm not suicidal.

I focus again, doing the same thing as before, but this time, I create the area of charged air further above me, and then push it away from me before releasing my magic.

A blinding flash of light crashes down, making me blink several times. And then blink again, just in case I didn't see correctly. The lightning bolt hasn't disappeared as it should have. Instead, it's hovering just above the ground, writhing and fighting against whatever is preventing it from disintegrating.

"Thor?" I call. "Are you doing this?"

"What do you mean?" He approaches me from behind but I'm too worried to turn away from the lightning.

"The frozen lightning bolt?" I ask him incredulously. "What else would I be talking about?!"

"Oh that. Yes, that's me. I wanted to show you what your magic can do in detail."

He says it as if this is nothing special. As if he didn't just freeze a fricking lightning bolt in time. Now that I know he's the cause of it, I feel a little less threatened. Hopefully, he'll stop it from exploding into my face.

I reach out with my magic, exploring what's actually happening.

"Close your eyes," Thor encourages me. "See it with your inner vision."

I think I prefer the Thor from the legends after all. This one is suddenly turning a little too weird.

But I do as he says - he is a God after all - and focus on the lightning bolt in front of me. It's harder to see magic with my mind that isn't my own. There are traces of my own still around, but they're scattered and hard to make sense of. It takes me a good while until I manage to find Thor's magic. It's very different from my own, much thicker and more solid. Mine is fluid and flexible, while his is rigid and not as easily changed. Maybe it's because his only has one purpose, while mine has to adapt to multiple elements.

It's as if a light is slowly turned on, exposing more and more of the big picture. The lightning bolt is surrounded by Thor's magic, held in place by a web of tiny magic tendrils that are growing into something that look like roots.

I step closer, examining one of the closest bits of the lightning. The magic is pulsating, with energy flowing out of the lightning and into Thor.

"Are you draining its energy?" I ask him in surprise.

"Look again," he replies simply.

Why can't he just tell me the answer? But then I remember, I used to do the same to the students back at university. People always remember knowledge they had to work out for themselves a lot better than content they were given to simply read.

This time, I focus on the connection Thor has built with the lightning bolt. There's the energy flowing towards him that I've already seen... and then... yes, there's energy flowing back from Thor into the lightning!

"You're keeping it in a stasis?" I ask. "You're not letting it deplete its energy?"

"Exactly. I can only keep it in that state for so long, so you may want to step back."

I jump away just in time for the lightning bolt to expand slightly and then ram into the ground, disappearing for good.

"A little more warning, next time?" I shout at Thor, running a hand over my eyebrows. They feel singed. I've already lost half of my hair, I'm in no rush to lose my eyebrows as well. Especially not now that they're perfectly curved. Somehow, I know that I'll never have to thread them again – those Goddess genes do come in handy.

Thor shrugs. "You got away in time. Do another one, bigger, this time."

I nod and watch as he retreats to the edge of a courtyard. I'm going to show him. He's the God of Thunder? Well, I'm the Demigoddess of Lightning. Kind of. Not really. But who cares.

I weave thick strands of magic through the air in front of Thor. I'm not even bothering to do it near me first and then pushing it towards him. He wants me to practice, so here I am, trying out new methods.

"I can see what you're doing!" he shouts and I cringe. Of course he does.

How can I surprise him if he can see my magic? Mmhm, there must be a way.

With a smile, I start gathering some magic behind him while still increasing the magic in front of him. Hopefully, he'll focus on that and miss what I'm doing behind him.

"You're wasting your time!" he calls. "Not seeing with your eyes, remember? I can feel what you're doing!"

Damn it. I should have thought of that myself.

But... he never said I'd have to do this on my own, right?

I send a mental nudge to Frost. I know he's nearby, I can feel him. Hopefully, I'm not distracting him from something important.

Our mental link is still mainly a way of nudging and pulling. The guys told me once that I would be able to talk to them, but that's not really how it works. I can send images through it, but they don't always reach their recipient. It's a bit of an unclear science. Sometimes it works, sometimes it doesn't. Luckily, the nudging always works.

Out of the corner of my eye, I see a door opening and Frost steps into the courtyard.

"Thor!" I shout, hoping to distract him. "What happens if my lightning was to touch water?"

"It would become quite explosive. Bigger. More effective. Why?"

Hopefully, Frost got the message.

"Just asking," I reply, suppressing a smirk. "Ready?"

Thor shrugs, as if he's bored already. I'm going to show him.

Frost is staying in the shadows, hiding behind a column lining the courtyard. He gives me a short nod to show that he understood. Let's do this.

"Ready, steady.... Go!" I shout, and let the lightning lose all around Thor. At the same time, Frost summons a water dome, imprisoning the God. When the lightning hits the watery cage, all hell breaks loose.

The water begins to steam and sizzle, and large cracks of lightning tear through the air. Sparks are flying, illuminating the steam which is becoming thicker, hiding Thor from view.

"You're playing a dangerous game, Godspawn," a voice suddenly says behind me. Thor is standing there, hands in his pockets, looking as relaxed as ever. His eyes however are glinting with delight. "But it's a very effective one. Well done. Anyone who couldn't teleport would be trapped – or dead."

That's when reality hits. This can kill people. Not just as a result of collapsing buildings like I did yesterday. No, this lightning can stop hearts, burn through flesh, erase enemies from existence.

As much as that makes me uncomfortable, I might need this in the future. I know there will be battles. I won't stay in the Palace and watch others be killed; I'll be out there, fighting with my Guardians, getting revenge for all Angus and the Morrigan have done to me and my family.

"How large can lightning be?" I ask Thor, thinking of how effective this would have been back at the Calanais Standing Stones. "How big of an area can it cover?"

"That solely depends on your magic and how much energy you want to throw into it. Lightning is powerful, but it also uses up a lot of your energy. I'd suggest keeping it as a last resort, because if you use a large amount of it, you'll be weak after."

"Let's imagine you were fighting a demon army." Thor raises an eyebrow but says nothing. "How many demons could you kill in one go?"

He thinks for a moment. "I think my record is about two hundred. You, with your power... maybe half of that. But as I said, be careful with it. Lightning has a mind of its own, and sometimes it takes more than it gives."

I nod. I'm well aware of that.

"Will you be fighting with us?" I ask him.

His expression changes and he gives me a tiny bow.

"Of course. I stand with Queen Beira, and now, with you. My soldiers are ready to assist whenever you need them. So are those of my brother. We've always stood with the Winter Realm and we will not stop now."

Warmth runs through me as I take in his words. I kind of want to hug him, but I'm not sure that's a good idea. He still isn't wearing a shirt, and Frost is watching. I don't want him to think that I fancy the God of Thunder. I mean, he's pretty, yes, but I have my Guardians. They're enough.

First though, I need to get one of them back on my side. Mission: Crispin is about to begin.

I stretch out a hand. "Thank you for the lesson, it's been very enlightening."

Thor roars with laughter.

Chapter Eight

Crispin isn't in his room, nor in my mother's, nor in the hospital wing.

I follow the bond that connects me to him, using it like a compass. It leads me upwards, high up one of the towers. I don't think I've ever been in this one.

The magic stairs transport me to the top faster than I could ever run up the steps. It also has the advantage that I'm not out of breath at all when I reach the top floor.

A curious sight awaits me. It looks like someone took a garden pavilion and transported it on top of a tower. Delicate columns are holding up a circular roof which is protecting a simple iron-wrought bench from the elements. Who had the idea of putting a bench on a tower? I wouldn't be surprised if it gets blown away by the next storm.

"Sit with me," a quiet voice says. Crispin. He's not on the bench and it takes me a moment to spot him. He's leaning against one of the pillars, his legs dangling down the side of the tower. One wrong move and he'd be falling. Is he feeling that depressed? No, he has wings, he'd just fly away. Still... I'm worried about him.

Carefully, I take a seat next to him, staying a bit further away from the edge.

"How are you?" I ask gently, but he doesn't respond. I'm tempted to reach out and put an arm around his shoulders, but I resist the temptation.

This is so awkward. It took me a long time to get Crispin to open up, and now it seems all that was for nothing. He's pulled up all his barriers again, and it's my fault.

I almost killed him.

I told him to write down what happened to him when he was a prisoner of the Morrigan. I made him go through that all again.

I didn't listen to him when he told me to stay away from Blaze's sparklies.

I made him open his heart to me, and then I crushed it.

"I'm sorry," I whisper. "I know I'm saying that far too late, but I'm really, really sorry."

He doesn't reply. I fold my hands, pressing my fingernails into my palms. That pain is only an echo of what's going on in my chest though. Crispin's silence is slicing through my heart, cutting me into little pieces. And I deserve it. I did the same to him.

"I hope you ignored what I told you to do back when... when the messenger came..."

"No," he says quietly, almost inaudible. "I wrote it all down and gave it to Tamara. It was necessary, you were right."

"No, I wasn't. You weren't ready, I was…"

"It's not all about you!" he suddenly shouts. "You don't get to decide when I'm ready. You don't get to apologise for something that isn't your fault!"

He still isn't looking at me, but that doesn't stop me from staring at him in confusion. What is he trying to say? That I'm self-obsessed? Selfish? Not caring about others? Whatever it is, it hurts.

Questions are running through my mind, but I'm too scared of his reaction to ask them. I don't want to hurt him even more. I've done enough already.

"You'll hate me," he mutters into the silence. "When you read it, you'll hate me."

"I could never hate you, Crispin," I whisper, still fighting against the urge to touch him. "I saw how she made you do things, you showed me."

"I didn't show you everything," he says bitterly. "You didn't see the worst of it. I don't deserve to be here. I should be rotting in a dungeon below the Palace, not sitting at the top of a tower with the heiress to the Winter throne."

He's confusing me. So he's not actually angry at me for cracking his skull? He's been avoiding me because he's drowning in self-doubt? I didn't expect that.

"Well, then I should be in the dungeon with you for attempted murder," I say, trying to make my voice jovial and light.

He doesn't smile though. "That was an accident. It could have happened to anyone."

"Ehm, no, it couldn't. How many Demigoddesses with weird powers do you know who've been addicted to unicorn sparklies?"

This time, his lips twitch a little. "True, you're unique. Do you still feel the urge to seek out Blaze?"

He's switched to his healer persona, but I'm letting him do that if it makes things easier for him.

"No, being in the Library cured that."

Finally, he turns to me with a look of curiosity.

"You went to the Library of Lives again?"

Of course, I forgot he wasn't there when I told the other three.

"Yes, but it was different this time." I give him a quick roundup of what happened, how I got to see my mother's book, how I decided to come back to this life.

"Do you think the Morrigan has a book there?" I suddenly ask when I've finished my tale.

"Yes, everybody has."

"Could we look at it? See what her plans are? Learn more about her past, perhaps, find something that will help us predict how she'll act?"

"It's a good idea, but the Library is a neutral place." Crispin sighs. "In times of war, neither party are allowed to look at the books of people on the other side. We wouldn't even be able to read one of her soldiers' books. It's frustrating, but it makes sense. Otherwise, the Library would become a target."

Pity. Just when I thought I'd found a new way to fight the Morrigan, it turns out other people have thought of that before. Figures. I'm new to all this, I'm not going to reinvent the wheel.

"I'm glad you came back," he says, as if that had ever been in question.

"Of course. I have things to do. And people I love."

I put a lot of emphasis on that last word, to make sure he knows that he's included in that.

And to be even more thorough, I finally put an arm around his shoulders and pull him closer. I've missed his touch, his scent.

"You should read what I gave Tamara," he says though and gently moves out of my embrace. "Come find me after if you still want to talk to me."

He gets up and jumps off the tower.

Moments later, he reappears, his golden wings fully unfolded, glistening in the sunlight. He does a loop and then disappears out of sight, leaving me with an empty feeling deep within my heart.

"You don't have to read this," Tamara tells me with a worried frown. "I've started making notes of the most important points and will present them at tomorrow's Council meeting."

I shake my head. "No, I need to do this. I've already seen Crispin's memories. How much worse can reading this be?"

With a gentle nod, she leaves me to it.

It turns out, a lot worse.

It's as if his voice is speaking in my head, telling me of all the suffering he went through. I can't switch off this inner monologue, and it makes it even more heartbreaking.

He killed children.

He tortured people for weeks.

He assassinated dozens of Guardians.

And worst of all, he slept with the Morrigan.

That's what finally makes my tears flow, after holding them back for a long time.

The Morrigan forced herself on him. It's clear from his words that he didn't want it. He doesn't say it, but I know that it was rape. She had him under her control and she took advantage of him.

When I've finished reading, I stumble off the chair and sit down on the floor in a corner. I need to think. I somehow need to work through this. There are so many emotions fighting in my chest, and I'm feeling bad because if this is how strong my reaction is to this, how much worse did Crispin feel while writing it all down?

I forced him to. He followed my commands, just like he was expected to.

I made him relive all the torture and violence, both what he received and what he did to others. I can't imagine him doing any of these things though. He was another person back then. Someone created to do terrible deeds. What's important is that he managed to fight it all and become a good person. Someone walking in the light, not in the dark the Morrigan created him in.

"Wyn?"

Frost enters the room and looks at me strangely when he notices me sitting in a corner.

"What's wrong? I felt your distress."

Did I accidentally use the bond? Or is this a new development?

"Crispin," I say simply and hold up the bunch of papers I've been reading.

"Oh. We told him not to write it. He knew that you weren't yourself when you ordered him to. But he said he wanted to do it anyway. There was no stopping him."

He sits down by my side and pulls me close. I melt into his touch, enjoying the warmth and comfort he's immediately giving me.

"Do you want me to read it so we can talk about it?" he asks but I shake my head.

"No, I don't think he would want that. I know why he wrote it, there is a lot of information in there that will help us. Tamara is going to compile a report by tomorrow. But her and I should be the only people reading it."

"Alright, but you know I'll be here if you want to talk about it."

I smile at him and cuddle against him. "I know. Thanks for being here."

His sea breeze scent slowly pulls me out of the dark feelings hammering in my chest.

"Do you want to kiss?" he asks.

"That's a very strange thing to ask. Are we back at primary school?"

He laughs. "I wasn't sure if you wanted that right now. I don't want to intrude."

I know what he means. I'm feeling bad about Crispin, and maybe I shouldn't be making out with another Guardian. But I need some time to think everything through before I talk to Crispin again. He might still be flying anyway.

"Kiss me, you silly Guardian."

"Of course, my Princess," he says in mock reverence, and cups my cheeks, pulling me close. When his lips touch mine, I focus on it with all I can, pushing back the memories of what I just read, at least for a while. I'm going to deal with them later.

For now, I need to heal, so I can heal Crispin.

Frost is gentle, so different from his brother. His kiss is soft and loving, sweet and slow. It's just what I need in this moment. He makes me feel good.

He removes one hand from my cheek and wraps it around my waist, readjusting my position until I'm sitting on his lap. Something hard is pressing against me from below and I smile against his kiss, knowing that this won't stay tame.

I concentrate for a moment, focussing on the door. With a click, it locks, and I know that a yellow shine will be showing around it. My mum told me that trick – now, nobody will be able to enter or listen in. Privacy is important in a Palace full of gossiping servants and courtiers.

Satisfied that we're going to be undisturbed, I slip my hands under his shirt and pull it up, breaking the kiss so he can take it off. I stare at his smooth, chiselled chest. He's been training a lot recently, and it's made his muscles even more defined. I run my hands over his abs, enjoying the feel of it. He's gorgeous, inside out.

"Take off your clothes," he says, his voice suddenly reminding me a lot of his brother's. It makes me shudder in anticipation.

I pull my shirt over my head and he sucks in a breath. My seamstress made me several sets of lingerie, and I'm wearing my new favourite bra, made of a fabric that's something of a mix between satin and lace. It's delicate but strong enough to hold my breasts in the perfect position.

I have to get up to get out of my shoes and my black linen trousers. His gaze heats when he sees my matching panties. They don't leave a lot to the imagination.

"Stay like that," he tells me when I've stepped out of my trousers. He gets on his knees and wraps his arms around my thighs, pulling me closer. He nudges me to spread my legs a little, giving him the perfect view. I shiver at the intensity of his gaze.

When his tongue touches my skin, I gasp. He licks at the spot just below my belly button, then slowly going down, grazing his teeth over the fabric of my panties. Why didn't he take them off? Why didn't I take them off?

He's such a tease.

His hands are wandering to my arse, squeezing at the same time as his tongue reaches that most special spot. Despite the fabric, his touch is electrifying, making me quiver as he begins to suck on my bud. Goosebumps are racing up my body and I tangle my hands in his hair, pressing him harder against my skin, encouraging him to suck harder.

He chuckles and begins to flick his tongue back and forth, giving me new waves of pleasure. My breath is getting faster. He knows exactly how to touch me; he's playing me like an instrument. His hands are massaging my cheeks, one finger precariously edging closer to my entrance.

I'm shaking. I won't last for much longer.

His finger draws little circles, teasing me, making me moan loudly.

His tongue is getting faster and faster, before he suddenly sucks in hard at the same time as entering me with his finger. I come apart, screaming and quivering. His other hand is on the small of my back, steadying me as I ride the waves of that most amazing orgasm.

With one final flick of his tongue, he leans back, looking at the soaked fabric of my panties.

I sink to my knees, falling into his arms. He holds me gently while my breath slowly returns to normal. How did he manage this with me still being half dressed?

He runs his fingers over my bare arms, caressing my skin. His touch is so full of love that I can't help but turn around and kiss him again, more passionate this time. I nudge his lips with my tongue until he opens his mouth, allowing me to enter. I soak in his taste, that sea salt scent, the feeling of the ocean. My magic is purring loudly in my chest, but I try and ignore her.

When I break the kiss, both of us are flushed and breathing heavily.

"Your turn," I whisper. "Take off your jeans. And whatever you're wearing underneath. If you're wearing something."

He gives me a suggestive wink and does as I asked. It doesn't surprise me that he's not wearing anything beneath his trousers. That seems to be a recurring theme with my men. They all seem to have an aversion to underwear.

His cock is hard, unsurprisingly.

"Sit down."

Again, he follows my command and sits by my side, his cock pointing up, ready for attention. I smile and lean down, pressing a gentle kiss on his tip. His skin is soft and warm, and even here, he has that sea salt taste.

I take him into my mouth, slowly, teasingly. He groans as I touch him with my tongue, before taking him in deeper. He's not as thick as his brother, but longer, I think. They're not twins in every place, apparently.

I wrap a hand around his balls, admiring once again the softness of his skin.

He groans at my touch. Just the encouragement I needed.

I move up and down on his cock, occasionally stopping to kiss the top. Pearls of moisture are collecting there and I lick them away.

"Wyn, you better stop," he warns me and I grin.

"Why would I do that?"

"I want to come inside you, not like this."

"Why not both?" I counter, surprising myself. I swallowed once before, with a boyfriend who I didn't actually like that much, and I hated it. But for some reason, I think that it would be different with Frost. He's my Guardian, he's so much more than a boyfriend. He's bonded to me, and his body is already bound to mine.

A knock on the door makes both of us jump a little.

"Your Highness, there's a messenger!"

I sigh in frustration, before removing the wards around the door so they can hear my answer.

"I'll be in the throne room in ten minutes!" I shout and immediately put the yellow glow back.

"Seems like you get your wish," I mutter to Frost and change my position, climbing on top of him until his cock is touching my entrance. "No time for more."

He laughs. "We can always continue once you've dealt with that messenger."

With that, he pushes up his hips and enters me in one long thrust.

"I've been wanting to do this for so long," he whispers as his thrusts are becoming quicker. "Just you and me, none of the others."

I put my hands on his chest and lower my pelvis, giving him even more access. He takes my breasts in his hands, massaging them gently.

"You should have said something," I reply, but it comes out as a moan as he suddenly pulls on my nipples.

"I knew I'd get my chance," he chuckles. "Now, do that scream again, the one with the moans and the shudders."

"Are you taking the piss?"

"Not at all. Scream for me, Princess. Show me how much you like it."

His hands leave my breasts and he grips my hips, pushing me down harder on his cock as he increases his rhythm even more. I'm close to the edge and let go of all that's holding me back.

Just like he wanted, I moan loudly, not caring how porn-like that sounds.

One more thrust and I'm pushed over the edge, contracting around him as I arch my back and scream in pleasure.

Moments later, he pushes in hard and shudders, before coming himself with a groan. He doesn't stop though, pounding again and again until I ride yet another wave of ecstasy, coming apart in his arms.

Chapter Nine

The messenger looks as exhausted as he is dirty. He's left muddy footprints all over the throne room and I pity the people who'll have to clean up later on.

"Give the man some water," I tell one of the servants and she scuffles off, returning moments later with a pitcher of water and a glass.

The messenger drinks it greedily.

"Thank you, my lady," he says with a deep voice. "I need to talk to the Queen."

I cringe. "Queen Beira is currently unavailable but I am her daughter, so you can tell me whatever message you had for my mother."

He blanches and does a hasty bow.

"Forgive me, I didn't know, Your Highness." He looks around the people watching us curiously. "You may want to listen to this message in private."

I nod and wave at Jonathan to clear the hall. The Lord Chamberlain looks like he's about to argue, but then does as he asks. He's never liked me – I don't think he likes anyone – but he's very aware that I'm well in my rights to give him orders.

He's the last to leave, but not before Arc slips into the room. The messenger is about to protest when my Guardian joins me at my side, but I quickly silence him.

"Arc will stay, he's trustworthy."

Arc pulls up an eyebrow as if he's questioning that statement, but says nothing.

"Now, what's your message?"

"I was sent by Flora and…"

Arc is suddenly in front of me, taking on a protective stance.

I'm confused. Who exactly is Flora? My knowledge of the Gods is still sketchy.

"Why are ye here?" Arc growls. "Everybody ken that the Spring Goddess is allied with Angus."

The messenger shrinks back a little. "That's why I'm here. She wants to talk about a switch of allegiances."

Arc doesn't change his stance. "Flora has been Angus's ally fer centuries. Why would she change that now?"

"You've not heard?" the messenger asks in confusion. "About Favonius?"

Another name I'm not familiar with. The problem is that I concentrated on learning more about the Celtic Gods. These two sound more like they're Roman. That's the problem with so many Gods that suddenly turn out to be real. There are far too many of them, but I never know which ones actually exist and which ones don't. It doesn't help that a lot of them go by several names, depending on what culture they're talked about. Thor for example is also known as Donar, Taranis, Indra and Perun. Yes, exactly, confusing.

"What's wrong with Fav?" Arc asks, his voice less aggressive now. It seems like he knows this Favonius guy, if he even has a nickname for him.

"He's dead," the messenger sighs. "Assassinated. There was a raven feather left on his body."

"Could someone please explain to me what's going on?" I push Arc out of the way and glare at him.

He clears his throat. "Favonius is... was the God of Wind. Flora is his wife, and the Goddess of Spring. Fav was a minor God who was once on our side, but when he fell in love with Flora, he started to support Angus like his wife. I'd not heard from him in a while."

"How was he killed?" I ask the messenger.

"Poison. One I've not seen before, but our healer said something about dragons."

"The poison of a black dragon?" I ask in shock and an ominous feeling sinks into my stomach when he nods.

"That's the same they tried to kill me with. It seems we have the same enemy."

The messenger is staring at me wide-eyed. He clearly didn't expect this.

"The raven feather is new though..." I mutter.

"The Morrigan," Arc replies darkly. "It's her sign. But why would she kill Fav? Did he do something ta oppose her?"

The messenger shakes his head. "I wouldn't know, but the Lady Flora wants to talk to you, I'm sure she can explain. I'm just the messenger."

"Will she come here? You can assure her that she'll have safe passage."

Arc grimaces and looks like he's about to say something, but then thinks better of it.

"I will let her know. She's waiting close to your Realm's border, so she could be here tomorrow, if that suits Your Highness."

"Yes, tell her to come. If we are to form an alliance, we better do it quickly."

The messenger bows deeply, visibly relieved that he can return to his mistress with good news. He turns to leave, but bows again before he exits through the large doors.

Once he's left, I turn to Arc.

"How powerful is Flora? Is she trustworthy?"

"She's the Goddess of Spring and fertility. Her element is earth, but I've never seen her use it, so I dinnae ken how strong she is. She's kept out of most battles, but if the Morrigan killed her husband, she might want ta get involved in this one."

I nod. "I'm going to talk to my mother about it. This means that either the Morrigan isn't actually working with Angus – she wouldn't attack one of his allies otherwise – or that she had a personal issue with Favonius. Hopefully Flora can tell us more about it tomorrow."

"What's worrying me is the poison," Arc says slowly. "It confirms that the dragons are involved, and that they're in league with the Morrigan. And the only dragon we could have asked has disappeared with Ada."

"Maybe we should search for her after all, now that things have changed. I'll see if Tamara can spare some people. Five people can't disappear just like that."

Another thought comes into my mind. "Arc, can you make a list of all the Gods and Goddesses supporting us. And then another of all those we definitely know are on Angus's side. If Flora is willing to switch sides, maybe she can bring some of her friends with her."

"Aye, will do. There are some neutral Gods as well, but I ken Beira was planning ta invite them all for talks. I think ye should do the same."

I cringe at the thought of inviting unknown Gods for a chat. I'm still not comfortable around them. The whole idea of Gods walking around us and behaving like normal humans... ehm, people... is still new to me.

Before I came to the Realms, Beira was the only Goddess I'd ever met, and she's different from them all. She's the Mother of Gods, she's not on the same level with the others.

Thor is a little aloof, but I think I could easily become friends with him. Some of the other minor Gods were just like people back at home, not intimidating at all. Others though... well, when I was suddenly confronted with Hades, the God of the Underworld, at one of my mother's balls, I bolted.

"I suppose so," I admit. "Can you ask someone to arrange that?"

"Aye. Dinnae worry, we'll be with ya all the way."

I hug him and breathe in his warm scent.

"I know, Arc. You don't know how much it means to me to have the four of you."

He chuckles. "Dinnae start being all mushy."

"Mushy?!"

"Mushy. Like mushy peas, but female."

I just shake my head and decide to not answer that. Men can be weird.

I spend the rest of the day arranging a search to be conducted for Ada and the dragon prisoner, before searching for Crispin. He's nowhere to be found, and he doesn't appear in the bedroom either when the four of us retire for the night. I snuggle up with the other three Guardians, but something is missing.

I try to fall asleep, listening to the deep breaths of my men. It's not working though. There's an ache in my chest, a sadness that isn't quite my own. Crispin is hurting. Is this what made Frost come and search me out earlier? Have we started feeling each other's pain?

Quietly, I get up, trying not to step onto one of the guys as I climb out of the bed. Storm lifts his head sleepily and I whisper "toilet", watching as he nods and falls asleep again.

I sneak out of the room, following the feeling in my chest. This time, it doesn't lead me up the tower, but outside into the freezing cold. I summon some warm air, wrapping my entire body in it like a cloak. My feet leave deep prints in the freshly fallen snow as I enter one of the gardens. White snowdrops are lining the pathways, joined by light blue flowers that look a bit like snowflakes with their jagged leaves.

"Crispin?" I call out into the darkness, still following the pain in my chest. The only light here is the moon reflected by the snow, painting the garden in a gloomy, pale yellow colour.

"You shouldn't be here," his quiet voice says from the shadows. I find Crispin lying on a bench in the centre of the garden, looking up at the night sky.

"Stop moping and talk to me."

I'm rougher than I intended to be, but I'm done with him evading me. Now that I know that he isn't actually angry at me, I'm more confident in stopping him from pushing me away.

"You didn't read it yet, did you." His voice is so full of loneliness and resignation that I can't help but bend down and kiss him. He doesn't respond though; his lips aren't moving like mine are.

Damn that man. Why can't he just believe that I love him no matter what he did in the past?

I stand up and put my hands on my hips, looking at him angrily.

"Listen to me. I read it. Yes, it was painful to read. Yes, I felt sorry for you. Yes, I still feel guilty for making you write this. But you know what? It didn't change anything about what you are to me. What I feel for you. Nothing can change that, and you know why? Because you're in here." I point at my chest, right where my heart is pounding hard. "And I'm in there." I touch his chest, feeling his own heartbeat. It's faster than mine.

"Now stop being like that and come back to me. I need you. No matter what you tell yourself, you're mine, and you always will be." I smile to soften my words a little. "You're my Crispy."

He chuckles bitterly. "I don't understand you. How can you say things like that after reading what I did? About what she did to me? I'm tainted, Wyn, and I'll never be whole. I'm not like the others. They can give themselves to you with all their heart, but I don't have much of my heart left. She took it from me, she made me erase my humanity. And I know that I could become like that again, if she was to capture me. I'd do the same things again. I'd kill. I'd torture. I'd climb into her bed if she commanded me to. Can you really love someone like that? A monster?"

He's sat up while he was speaking and tears are shining in his eyes, reflecting the moonlight.

I go on my knees and take his hands in mine, squeezing them hard. "You're not a monster. And that bitch is never going to get her hands on you again. I'll kill her before she even gets close to you. You're free of her, Crispin. You're no longer alone. You have me, and the guys. You don't have to fight your demons alone."

He looks down at me and a tear slides down his cheek.

"Even if the demons are real?"

I smile and squeeze his hands again. "Even then. Especially then. Real demons can be killed. We'll deal with her and then you'll be free."

Finally, he gives me a tiny smile and wipes away his tears.

"You really are a Princess, Wyn. No, you're a Queen."

Chapter Ten

When I wake up this time, all four of my Guardians are in the same bed with me. Crispin joined us after our talk in the garden, and the others made space for him without saying a word. It almost feels like before it all came to pieces.

Today, I'm going to meet an enemy for the first time. A political one, that is, I'm not counting all the demons we slayed. Those were enemies on an entirely different level. For them, it was a hack and slash tactic. For Flora, I need to use a different method.

First though, I want to hear what she has to say. Maybe there's a reason why the Morrigan killed the Spring Goddess's husband. That would make it easy to get her on our side. I can promise her that we'll bring the Morrigan to justice – something Angus probably hasn't been able to give Flora.

I'm going to meet a lot of Gods in the next few days. Flora today, then several of the neutral Gods tomorrow. Tamara insisted that we throw a party for them; she says that's the only way to make sure that they'll all attend. She's also invited some of the Gods we know are on our side, in the hope that they'll help persuade the neutral ones that we're the good guys.

I can't imagine why anybody would fight on the Morrigan's side. She's evil through and through, and she doesn't care about others. She's only interested in her own power.

And Angus... well, I'm told that most Gods supporting him do so out of habit. They were either created by him or have been his allies for centuries or longer. For them, it might look like just another war between Angus and Beira, and not like the fate of the Winter Realm is at stake. If either Angus or the Morrigan were to seize my mother and her power, it would result in chaos. The balance needs to be upheld, no matter the cost.

I grimace. Look at me, making pompous statements like that. I really am turning into a Princess. A Princess with a lot of responsibilities.

I should really get up and start on my to-do list. I've only set foot into my mother's office once, and I know that a lot of tasks are waiting there for me. Things to sign, letters to reply to, budgets to approve. I think Tamara is dealing with most of the minor issues, but sometimes, a Royal signature is needed. I have no idea how she does it all. Tamara is a force of nature.

I yawn loudly to show the guys that it's time to start the day. An arm snakes around my waist and pulls me close. Storm.

"We need to get up," I protest, but he simply presses me against his warm body and wraps his other arm around me.

"Just making sure you're okay," he mutters with a sleepy voice.

"I'm fine, why are you doubting that?"

Frost chuckles. "It's his excuse to hold you. I think I need to check on you next."

"Guys, I don't have time for this," I sigh, although my body is very much protesting against my words. I want to have them all close, touching me.

"Can we do this in a circle while standing?" I suggest. "That's quicker."

"Do you mean us standing and you on your knees?" Storm whispers into my ear and I feel my cheeks flush.

"No, I mean a hugging circle. Just hugging. Friendly hugging. As friends. You know, without any sexual bits that take time."

The guys roar in laughter.

"Maybe we should show her that it doesn't always need to take a lot of time," Frost snickers, and I blush even more. "We can skip the foreplay."

"What did I do to deserve this?" I sigh dramatically. "But as your Princess, I order you to stop touching me."

"Aw, I love when she pulls rank," Arc chuckles. "So cute."

With an evil grin, I send a bit of very cold air underneath the covers and between his legs. He yelps and jumps up, tangling himself in the duvet and almost falling out of bed.

"Ehm, what just happened?" Crispin asks cluelessly, and I give him the same treatment. Just like Arc, he jumps and cries out. The two brothers decide that they don't want to find out what I'm doing, and with a sigh, they join the others. Now I'm the only one on the large bed, and I enjoy watching them standing naked all around me.

I should make them walk around naked more often. They're so pretty in all the right places.

"Are you ogling us?" Frost asks, lifting his eyebrows. "That's not very polite."

"If you don't like me staring, you should put on some clothes."

"Take a good look." Arc points at his half-erect cock. "This one will be waiting for you underneath my kilt all day."

Just when my cheeks had returned to a normal colour... Oh well. I really need to stop blushing this much.

I turn away from them and climb out of bed, walking towards my massive wardrobe. It's full of dresses, but I also managed to get the seamstress to make me some shirts and trousers. I know they all like wearing dresses here, but that's not really my style.

Today though, I should wear something impressive. Something that shows power and status.

In the end, I decide on a dark blue dress made from a shiny, heavy fabric that's clinging tightly to my body. Golden thread decorate the neckline and sleeves, the only adornment on the otherwise simple dress. Still, I think the absence of any frills and unnecessary decorations shows I take our visitor seriously, while the gold and the quality of the fabric are proof of my status.

I add a brooch with my mother's coat of arms. Only members of the Royal family are allowed to wear that – which basically means my mum and me. She gave me an entire set of that jewellery, including a heavy necklace, but for today, the brooch will be enough.

Ready and dressed, I run my fingers through my hair. I'm still not used to missing half of it.

"I think I need a hairdresser," I sigh. "I can't go to meet Flora like this, and I don't want to continue wearing scarves. People are going to ask questions about that soon."

"You could shave off the other side," Crispin suggests. "And then braid the remaining hair. It will make you look like a badass warrior."

"Or shave it all off. It might set a trend," Frost adds. "If it helps, I can shave mine too."

I glare at him. "Don't you dare. Keep your hair the way it is now. The only one allowed to get a haircut is Storm."

"Why me?" the Guardian in question asks. "Don't you like my hair?"

"I do, but it would be fun if you had the same haircut as your brother. You could play tricks on people... you know, like twins are supposed to do. But you'd have to get rid of that scowl first."

"I don't scowl."

"Yes, you do. Now get dressed. Arc, you're the only one ready, would you mind finding me a hairdresser somewhere? There must be someone in this Palace."

"I could get ya some scissors..."

"Hairdresser. Now."

I'm wearing a wig. A freaking wig. In the end, that seemed like the best option. I wasn't quite brave enough for the warrior Princess option.

The wig almost looks like my real hair, but I can't help running my hand through it self-consciously.

"Don't worry, it looks good," Frost reassures me as we walk towards the throne room.

He's assigned to me today – Storm is working with Gwain, Crispin is looking after my mother and Arc is helping Tamara with spy stuff. Storm tried to insist on two Guardians being with me at all times, but he realised that everybody is too busy for that.

"Have you ever met Flora?" I ask him, mentally going through what I read on her yesterday evening before going to bed.

"Only once, but I don't really remember it. She didn't seem very interesting at the time. There was gossip about her hooking up with Fav, but I've never really cared for all of that."

"Hooking up? That's a strange way of describing the relationships of Gods."

"They're not as godly as people think," he explains. "They all have their faults and weaknesses. It's easiest to see Gods as just another species, like Guardians and humans. They might have a bit more power, but that doesn't make them any more intelligent."

"I don't think most Gods would agree with that statement." Tamara is waiting for us in front of the large doors leading to the throne room. She's grinning widely at Frost's statement, as if she agrees entirely with him. I suppose she has a lot of dealings with Gods, whether they're aware of it or not. She has spies in all of their Realms who likely tell her of the unsavoury things those Gods are up to.

"Darling, you look lovely," she tells me, looking up and down my dress. "The brooch is a nice touch. Shall I get you the diadem as well?"

I shake my head, worried that the diadem might make the wig slide off my head. Unlikely, but I don't quite trust that hairy thing yet.

"Flora is waiting for you inside. I've taken the liberty to make everyone else leave, except for a few guards, of course. Is there anything else you need from me?"

"How's my mother?"

I didn't have time to check on her before coming here. It makes me feel bad, but I know that she would prefer me to focus on my Royal duties rather than sit by her bedside.

"Doing well. Crispin just arrived when I left, so she's in good hands. Don't worry, you'll do fine. See you at the Council meeting."

She smiles and hurries off down the corridor, leaving Frost and me alone.

I take a deep breath.

"Let's do this."

F lora is waiting by the throne, her back to the door, but she turns when she hears us enter. Frost stays close to the entrance, watching me just like the rest of the guards who are scattered around the room. Seems like I need to do this on my own.

The Goddess of Spring gives me a deep courtesy, waiting in that position until I get close to her. I admire her courtesy skills; mine are still severely lacking. I almost fell over once or twice, but luckily, they don't expect a Princess to do a lot of those anyway.

"Please stand," I tell her and she looks up at me, showing me her face for the first time.

She's beautiful, no, stunning. Her porcelain skin highlights her golden eyes and rosy cheeks, framed by shiny blonde curls. Her hair is held back with a mayflower wreath, the white petals almost the same colour as her flawless skin.

Her ivory dress is almost translucent, wrapping around her body like a toga, exposing a lot of her exquisite figure. She must be freezing though, this really isn't the kind of clothing to wear in the Winter Realm.

She reminds me of a white orchid, delicate but with an inner strength. Very fitting, given her name.

"Your Highness," she says in a soft voice, almost a whisper. "Thank you for seeing me."

That's when she looks straight into my eyes and I recognise something very familiar. Grief. Bottomless sadness.

I decide to forego the formalities and lead her to one of the alcoves on the right side of the room, rather than up to the throne.

Two stone benches are opposing each other, separated by a small table that the nobles like to use to play chess or some other games. Flora seems a little surprised by the breach of protocol, but she slides onto one of the benches with more elegance than I will ever possess.

I take my seat opposite her, not quite sure how to begin. I'm like a fish out of water who's been stuffed into a dress and told to behave regal.

"I'm sorry for your loss."

"Thank you, Your Highness."

That's the easy bit out of the way. Deciding to forego any pleasantries and small talk, I jump straight in.

"Your messenger said that your husband was murdered? With the poison of a black dragon?"

Her eyes widen slightly, but she stays poised.

"Yes, Your Highness. We found him in the morning, a raven feather on his chest. There was blood on his lips and the healer later found traces of the poison on his tongue. He says it was in something Fav ate…"

She pauses but then blurts out, "I think it was meant for me. I was late for dinner so he began to eat on his own, and I got myself a snack from the kitchens before going to bed. Maybe he took something from my plate."

She breaks off and swallows hard.

"Is it more likely that the Morrigan wanted to kill you rather than your husband?" I ask gently. She cringes at the mention of the Morrigan but regains her composure quickly.

"I was given information," she says slowly. "One of my spies found something by accident… she told me, but she was killed at the same time as my husband. I'm the only one who knows what she found."

That's making things a lot more interesting.

"Your husband never knew?"

"No, he didn't get involved much in business affairs." She sniffs. "There was no reason for anyone to kill him."

"What's the information, if it's worth killing for?"

"I want protection for me and my family. My soldiers will fight in your war, but the ordinary people of my Realm need to be protected. My home is much closer to the Summer Realm, so it's likely that Angus will want to take revenge on me once he finds out that I've been to see you."

"Why would Angus want revenge? Surely you're not the only one thinking about leaving his side?"

"It's not that." She pauses, then looks me straight into the eyes, a hint of steel showing in hers. "My spy saw him meet with the Morrigan. And I can tell you where."

Chapter Eleven

"We don't have the manpower to protect another Realm!" Magnus shouts over the noise. "Nor do we have the resources."

"She might be able to give us vital information about where we can find the Morrigan," Storm counters, not even bothering to raise his voice. "If we know where she's hiding, we have the advantage. We can attack her before she has gathered all her forces."

"Who says that Angus met the Morrigan in her hiding place? They could have chosen a random spot in neutral territory! Flora might be bluffing to get our help."

The treasurer's face has turned red. As much as I don't like the man, I have to at least address his doubts.

"Gwain, is what Magnus says true?" I turn to the Master of Arms on my left. "Do we not have enough soldiers to protect her Realm?"

"If she didn't have an army of her own, then it would be a problem. She has a large number of soldiers herself, though. Nowhere near the size of our own or Angus's force, but still quite impressive for a Realm her size. I don't believe that she's trying to get that kind of protection. What she wants is that you publicly announce her as your ally. That means that if someone was to attack her, you'd defend her – hopefully a good deterrent for anyone to mess with her."

I nod. "That makes sense. How will Angus react if I ally with Flora?"

Storm snickers. "He won't be happy."

"He'll regret that the first assassination attempt didn't work," Tamara says, her lips twitching. "I'm sure he was aware of the attempt on Flora's life, if it was indeed aimed at her and not at her husband. He'll likely try again, even once she's divulged her secret to us. He needs to show both his allies and his enemies that anyone who betrays him will have to suffer the consequences."

"Does that mean we should keep Flora here, for her protection?"

Gwain nods. "Yes, that would be advisable. Times have shown that the Palace is no longer as impenetrable as we would like, but it's still the safest place for the Spring Goddess. I can send some of my officers into her Realm to help with the defences."

"And who's going to pay for that?" Magnus fumes, still standing while everyone else is seated around the large table.

"You," I tell him, hiding a smile. "The Royal coffers should be there to help the defence of the Realm, direct and indirect. What's the problem? Are we running out of money?"

He wrings his hands, obviously annoyed that I'm not taking him seriously.

"No, Princess, we have enough resources."

"Then what's the big problem? I'm having trouble understand, Treasurer."

"We should focus on our own first!" he bursts out. "Let Flora look after herself, we have enough to do protecting our own Realm."

The room falls deadly silent.

"Get out," I say in a quiet, measured voice. Inside I'm seething, but I'm not letting him know that. Who does he think he is? "This is not the way I'm going to rule. I'm not going to put on blinkers and ignore what's happening outside of this Realm. If someone comes to us for help, we will assist as best as we can. Only if we all stand together will we be able to win against our enemies."

He shoots me a hateful glance, then slams closed the door behind him.

I sigh deeply. "Tamara, do we have someone else who could take our beloved treasurer's role?"

I know I have them all shocked. They didn't expect me to send away one of the Council members, and they certainly didn't expect me to want to replace him. Well, look again, boys. Once my mother is back on her feet, she can always reinstate him, but for now, he's to stay out of my sight. I've never liked him, and I won't be able to suffer his racist attitudes.

"His assistant, Leo, is a bright young fellow," Tamara says slowly. "He doesn't have Magnus's experience, but he's clever and innovative."

"Have him come to me later," I order. "Let's see if we can't bring some fresh minds into this Council."

That has them all sit up straight. They're probably thinking whether I might replace some of them as well. As if I'm planning to do that. Magnus didn't really leave me a choice. I couldn't ignore statements like that.

"Shall we proceed? I will talk to Flora later, and maybe Gwain and Storm might want to be present. But first, is there any other business we need to discuss?"

Zephyr lifts his hand, almost shyly. Is he suddenly scared of me?

"Lucifer has sent a message. Your mother gave him the task to find out more about the black dragon poison back when you were almost killed. He said he wasn't able to enter the Dragon Realm. They've barricaded themselves, no one is able to enter or leave."

"Are they trying to protect themselves from the coming war?" I ask.

"I doubt it," Gwain says, his fingers playing with his beard as he thinks. "There's something else going on there. I wish we had the time to figure it out, but for now, I think our priorities need to lie elsewhere."

"Agreed. It doesn't seem like they will help us, but as long as they don't do anything threatening, let's ignore them."

Zephyr nods and makes a note on one of the many papers he has lying in front of him. I'm still not entirely sure of what exactly his role is in the Council. There are no birds here that he could be keeping, and most messages are sent via mental links or messengers. If a Guardian can fly a lot faster than birds, why use courier pigeons.

He seems to assist others a lot. I've seen him take orders from Tamara and help Algonquin in the library - but that may be just an excuse to spend time with his boyfriend. I don't think everyone is aware that the two of them are a couple, but to me, it's pretty obvious.

If my mother has Zephyr on her Council, there must be a reason for it. He must be helpful somehow, even if it's not obvious at first.

I look around the room. "Anything else we should discuss?"

"I have sent scouts to the Northern Gate," Gwain says, reminding me of our discussion yesterday. "We should hear back from them by tomorrow at the very latest. There's a snowstorm brewing, so their progress is slower than I'd hoped."

"Good, inform me as soon as you hear from them, whether it's good news or bad."

"Several Gods have announced that they're coming to your party tomorrow," Tamara tells me with a gleeful smile. "I've let the Palace staff know to prepare a banquet."

I shudder internally. I thought that now that we were at war, I wouldn't have to go to any more balls and festivities. No such luck. The Gods want to be entertained, and so entertain them we will. Hopefully, it will end up being an effective way of finding out who's supporting us and who isn't.

"Can you prepare a list for me with all who're going to attend?" I ask her, very aware that I will likely not have heard of most of them. Hopefully, I'll have some time tonight to do some research, or get one of the guys to explain who's important and who I can ignore.

"Of course, consider it done. Thor will be there as well, and he's bringing his daughter too. Not sure why but he wanted me to let you know."

Oh no. He wants me to do some girl to girl chat with her. This couldn't come at any worse time, but he's one of our closest allies and I can't afford to upset him.

"Are we all done here?" I get up and look at them with barely hidden impatience. "I have a Spring Goddess to meet. Gwain, Storm, you're with me."

A Palace guard leads us into one of the gardens. I'm a bit surprised, I'd have thought Flora would have been more comfortable in a room with a fireplace, not out here in the cold. But when I see her sitting amongst the flowers, the snow around them melted and new colour breathed into their petals, I understand why she's here. She's the Goddess of Spring, she's got a connection to nature. I could swear that there are some new flowers among the ones familiar to me. Did she actually make them grow in the few hours she's been our guest?

She seems deep in thought and doesn't even realise that we're here until we're standing right in front of her.

She looks up and I give her a friendly smile.

"Flora, I'd like to introduce you to Gwain, our Master at Arms, and Storm, his second in command. Both, meet Flora, the Goddess of Spring."

"A pleasure," Gwain says smoothly, while Storm gives her a sharp nod.

"We've met. Sorry about Fav."

Even for Storm, that's very brusque, but I'm letting it go for now.

"Shall we go inside?" I suggest, not so much caring about the cold but more about the eyes and ears that could be hiding in the garden. I much prefer a room where I can spell the doors so nobody can listen in.

I lead them into a random sitting room - one of dozens or even hundreds in this Palace - and carefully close the door, adding some magic to make it soundproof.

Once everybody has taken a seat, I get my thoughts in order. This is my first big test at diplomacy and negotiation. I better not mess this up.

""Flora, we've just had our Council meeting and came to a decision."

Slow start, raise expectations, see her reaction. That's my strategy. No idea if it makes sense. But it's better than blurting out everything, which would be the non-strategic way.

She raises a perfectly manicured eyebrow but waits for me to continue.

"Some of my advisors were sceptical about the benefit for us, should we announce that you're under our protection."

I'm not mentioning that the obvious advantage for us would be the support of her army. She knows that, I know that, but let's pretend we don't.

"However, I did manage to persuade them that we can make this into a mutually beneficent arrangement. We will publicly announce that you are now our ally and that you and your

Realm are under our protection. We will house you here at the Palace, where you will be safest. You'll have whatever you need and the support of the Palace staff. Gwain will send some of his officers to your Realm to coordinate with your own army, so that we can unify our approach to the defence of both our Realms. Does that sound good so far?"

"It does, Your Highness."

She smiles and I give her a quick smile back. I don't know why she calls me highness all the time. She's a Goddess, I'm only half one. Theoretically, she's miles above me.

"In return, you will provide us with information about the Morrigan and Angus. You will also pledge your army's support should we need it if the Winter Realm gets attacked. Again, the details can be arranged with Gwain. I would also like you to give us some information on who is supporting Angus, and who might be willing to switch sides. If there are others in a similar position, we need to know."

Flora nods several times, her hair bopping up and down.

"Agreed. I have one more request, though," she says, her voice firm but friendly. "My husband hasn't been cremated yet. I would like his funeral to be here, in the place where he was created."

I swallow hard, remembering once again how much death has been all around me recently. The Morrigan is killing people and we can't do anything about it. As long as my father is still alive... I wish I knew for certain that he's alright. That's the wrong word though. Of course he isn't alright. He'll never be again. My mum's dead, killed before his eyes, and mine, in a way. I can still hear her screams echoing in my mind.

"Of course, I'll ask one of my colleagues to make arrangements," Storm answers for me, giving me a knowing look. I could do with a hug right now, but I first need to deal with Flora. First, Princess duties, then I'm allowed Wyn emotions.

"Do you have any other family you'd like to join you here?" I ask the Goddess, not expecting it but aiming to be polite nonetheless.

"No," Flora says quietly. "Unlike Beira, us other deities aren't allowed children."

I swallow again, trying not to take it personally. She's grieving, and of course she'd like to have someone to help her get through it. Maybe she has friends among the Gods coming to the ball tomorrow. That might cheer her up a little.

"Gwain, would you mind drawing up a contract to put what we just discussed into writing?" I ask the Master of Arms.

"Of course, Your Highness. I will present it to both of you to sign before dinner. By then I'll also be able to give you a list of the officers I recommend to travel to the Spring Realm. Storm, let me know if you have anyone you think should go."

"Flora, will you be able to give us the information you promised?" I ask, trying not to sound too impatient. She's able to get us closer to the Morrigan, but the longer it takes for us to find out more, the less the chances that the Morrigan might still be where Angus met her.

She frowns.

"Once we've signed the agreement. Don't take this personally, but I'm doing this for the citizens of my Realm, not for myself. I need to make sure that they're safe before I give away my only bargaining chip."

I nod. "I understand. Believe me, I'd do the same."

She gives me a tense smile and gets up graciously. "Is there a room I could retire to? I'd like to freshen up a bit."

Between a quick snack from the kitchens, a hug with Storm (and a bit more than just a hug) and several hours in my mum's study, I'm ready to meet Flora again. For the third time today. If this continues like that, she might soon become my best friend. Or at least my best ex-enemy.

I ring the magical bell on my mother's desk and a moment later, a servant enters. Being a Princess does have its advantages.

I ask her to ask Flora, Gwain and Storm to join me, and to get some drinks and nibbles from the kitchen. My stomach has been growling for the past hour, and who knows how long this is going to take. Dinner might not be in the near future.

"Frost, feel free to leave, Storm will be here any moment."

My Guardian has been sitting in a corner, reading. He must be bored by now, following me around all day. I've been very tempted to give in to his charm and spend some quality time with him rather than with state affairs, but I know my mother is depending on me. I'll make sure to make up for it in bed tonight.

"I'll stay, if that's alright. I've met Flora before and would quite like to say hello."

Yey, another Guardian to give me mental support! I wish I had all four of them here. Their presence soothes me, even if they're just in the room like Frost right now.

Gwain and Flora arrive at the same time. Like a gentleman, Gwain pulls her chair back and waits until the Goddess has sat down before he takes a seat himself. My mother's study is large, and not only contains the desk I'm sitting on, but also a small conference table with five comfortable chairs around it. Bookshelves line the wall, but I've not had any time yet to take a closer look. I assume it's all connected to the politics and history of the Realm – I'm not really expecting my mother to read romance novels in her office. Or ever.

Maybe I should bring her some books to her bedroom. Some light fiction, something to make her smile. I wish I had my own books here with me. They're still back in Edinburgh, if nobody has plundered the house after my parents were kidnapped. I can't imagine demons being interested in fantasy novels – they *are* fantasy, after all – but you never know. Chesca was an unusual demon, who's to say there aren't more like her.

Storm is the last to arrive, together with a plate of hot rolls and small cakes.

"I met the servant on the way," he says with a large grin while munching on a cheese scone. "I decided to help him carry this."

"That's very kind of you," I tease. "Such a gentleman."

Flora is clearly trying to hide a smile. I'm not sure if she knows that Storm and I are together. Frost is back in his corner with a book, after saying hello to the Goddess when she entered. I can feel his presence however, our bond sending warmth through me.

Gwain clears his throat and lays a stack of paper on the table, together with two old-fashioned quills and a pot of ink. On my mother's table she has normal pens and pencils, but apparently, we're going traditional for official occasions. I hope I won't embarrass myself by leaving ink splats all over the contract. That would be so like me.

The Master of Arms hands both me and Flora a copy and I'll read through it. There's a lot of different paragraphs and clauses on there, in complicated, elaborate language. I assume though that if Gwain wrote this, that it's all in the interest of the Realm and won't have any clauses in there that I should worry about.

"I gave a copy to your mother as well," he says with a knowing smile. "She has approved it all and is happy for you to sign in her stead."

I feel a twinge of annoyance at hearing that second sentence. In front of Flora, this might sound like I didn't have full authority to negotiate with her before, and that I need my mother's permission. She explicitly told me that I don't – I can come to her for advice at any time, but I'm perfectly fine to make all my own decisions. I'm proud that she trusts me this much.

"This looks good to me," Flora mutters, her eyes flicking over the document. "I'm happy to sign it, if you are, Your Highness."

"Call me Wyn," I say pleasantly, and sign the contract with a flourish – more accident than intentional, but they don't need to know that the quill almost slipped from my hand. I hand my sheet of paper to Flora and take hers in return, signing it a bit more carefully this time.

Once we've both put the contracts on the table, I smile at the Goddess.

"You're now officially an ally of the Winter Realm. I'll be announcing it at the ball tomorrow, and I'll have our Master of the Wings spread the message to our other allies and friends. Gwain, have you chosen who you're going to send to the Spring Realm?"

He nods and hands me a list of names unfamiliar to me.

"Storm and I have agreed on all of those. One of them, Jula, has mind magic and will be able to communicate with us here in the Palace should the need arise."

I know how rare it is for Guardians to have this magic, and by the surprised look on Flora's face, she knows it as well. This is a big gesture and I'm sure she appreciates it.

"Thank you, Gwain. Hopefully by the time the news reaches Angus, they'll already be in Flora's Realm, ready to take action if needed."

"Of course, my Princess, I'll dispatch them as soon as we're done with this meeting."

I smile. "Then we better get this done quickly. Flora, you've got all the assurances from us you requested. Now it's your turn."

She nods hesitantly. "I sent one of my messengers to Angus to give him an invitation to a party Fav wanted to throw. It was something trivial, but still... it ended up being so much more."

She pauses for a moment and I know that she must be thinking of her husband, and how this party invitation resulted in his death.

"Just before he reached Angus's palace, he saw a group of people flying in the opposite direction. He thought he'd spotted the Summer God, so he followed them rather than continuing on to the palace. Somehow, he managed to stay out of sight, or at least they didn't notice him. They flew all the way to the Eastern edge of his Realm, where they landed and seemed to be waiting for someone. My messenger was about to descend and speak to them – by now he knew for sure that it was Angus down below – but then someone else arrived. A woman appeared out of thin air, wrapped in a black cloak, with hair as black as the night and skin as pale as the moon."

"The Morrigan," I whisper, remembering the memories Crispin showed me. She'd been beautiful, stunning, except for the coldness in her eyes and the cruel smile on her lips.

"Yes. The Goddess of Death and Darkness. Of course, my messenger was far too scared to land or get closer, so he didn't hear what they said. Only at the end of their conversation, the wind suddenly turned and he heard one single sentence: See you at Tioram."

"Tioram? Where's that?" I ask, struggling to remember where I've heard that name before.

"Surely she didn't mean Castle Tioram on Earth?" Storm frowns. "That's the only Tioram I know."

"I hadn't even heard of that castle," Flora admits. "But I asked my librarian and he showed me a map of a place called Scotland. Tioram is a ruined castle on a tidal island, and humans aren't allowed to go there. It sounds like a great hideout, but I don't get why a Goddess would stay on Earth. Our powers are weak there and it becomes painful if we stay too long."

She shrugs. "Of course I sent some scouts there. I needed to be sure that Angus was really working with the Morrigan. I've not liked his methods for a while, but he's my creator and Spring and Summer have always stuck together. I ignored the things he did, and tried to focus on my own Realm, keeping out any trouble he might bring with him. I even harboured some people who'd fallen afoul of Angus, protecting them from him. But I never outright went against him – until now. I can't believe he's working with the Goddess of Death. It's extreme even for him… everybody knows the story of what she did to that Guardian she created. How she made him kill children. It's disgusting."

I smooth my expression, carefully hiding the effect her words have on me. She's heard about Crispin. I didn't know his tale was that widely known. But of course, I assume Beira doesn't intervene in the business of other Gods very often, not unless it's necessary. The news that she banished the Morrigan must have spread like wildfire back then.

"What did your scouts find?" Gwain asks Flora and I pull myself out of my thoughts.

"They never returned. The next day, my husband was dead."

She blinks several times, trying to hide her threatening tears.

Gwain strokes his beard – he always does that when he's deep in thought.

"That means that someone definitely is at Castle Tioram, unless they were captured on route. Maybe Angus or the Morrigan saw your messenger after all and were monitoring your moves? Either way, we need to go to that castle."

"I'd be happy to put a team together," Storm volunteers. "And I'll join them."

"I'll go too," I say immediately, followed by three loud nos. I turn around and look at Frost, who's glaring at me.

Flora chuckles softly. "That's the price we have to pay as rulers: others get to have all the fun."

Her words take me by surprise. I didn't think she'd be someone who considers exploring a ruined castle and potentially fighting a Goddess 'fun'. Maybe I've misjudged her.

"She's right, Wyn," Storm says calmly, but his eyes are burning with emotion. "You're our Princess, hell, you're the Heiress. The one in charge. We need you here, where you're safe. There's a reason Beira has an army and doesn't fight the battles herself. If something happens to our ruler, the entire Realm will be thrown into chaos."

"You're not strong enough to fight the Morrigan though."

He smiles. "Neither are you. We're not intending to fight her. This is a scouting mission. If we find her there, we'll return and make plans how to attack with our full force. If not, then... well. Let's have Algonquin look for any other places called Tioram. Maybe there's somewhere in one of the Realms with that name."

"I'll let him know," Frost announces from behind me. "It's Arc's turn to accompany Wyn tomorrow, so I'll be able to help the librarian."

"I hope you find her there," Flora says. "And once you do, let me know. I have a word or two to say to that bitch. I may be the Goddess of Spring, but even newly grown flowers have strength. I'm not weak, I'm life, while she is death. I will fight alongside you."

She smiles and gets up.

"And now goodnight, Your Highness, gentlemen."

She leaves the room while the rest of us mutter good night, taken aback by her sudden show of strength.

She's right. She's spring, and spring is life. It's good to have her on board.

Chapter Twelve

"Come, we need to talk." Crispin's voice wakes me from deep sleep and it takes me a moment to fully regain my bearings. I'm in bed, deep breaths around me signalling that the men are here with me. Crispin is crouching on the floor by the bed so that his head is on the same level as mine.

"I need to talk to you, it's urgent," he whispers. His face is hidden in the dark, but his voice is unmistakable.

I sigh and lift the heavy arm lying on top of my ribcage. Storm grunts in his sleep.

"Crispin wants to talk, I'll be back soon," I tell him quietly, unsure if he's actually awake. I climb out of bed and follow Crispin, who's already waiting for me by the door. Moonshine is streaming through the high windows, illuminating his blond hair.

"What's going on?" I ask once he's closed the bedroom door behind us.

"Not here, let's talk outside."

Is it something the others aren't allowed to hear?

Curiously, I follow him as he leads me into one of the smaller courtyards. There's nobody around, not even guards. We're so deep inside the Palace that nobody expects enemies here. The sky is protected with shields, stopping anyone trying to fly in without permission. I smile at the memory of when I first arrived here. There was that weird man, Bertrand, who didn't want to let us in. I never saw him again. Did Tamara punish him for interfering with the barrier?

Crispin stops in the middle of the courtyard and I almost bump into him. I summon one of the glow balls and make it hover above our heads so I can look at my Guardian.

He's looking at me curiously, as if he's trying to make sense of me. Did I do something strange? Was this the first time he's seen me summon a light? Do I have dirt on my face?

His eyes are dark, even though the light is now shining straight at him. I've never seen them so dark. They have almost none of their usual blue left, only black and streaks of silver around his pupils.

"Is everything okay?" I ask him, wondering if maybe he's ill.

"Yes, everything is fine. Perfectly fine. I didn't think it to be this easy."

Suddenly, his arm is around my waist and something presses against my throat. Something that isn't actually there. I don't feel anything on my skin, but my windpipe is close to getting crushed. I try to breathe, get that pressure away from me, but it's not working.

I fight against Crispin's hold, struggling to get his hands off me. What the fuck is he doing? Is he having another flashback, like back at Chesca's cottage? Or is this a test and he wants to see how well I defend myself?

Well, he's going to get the fight he seems to want.

The pressure on my throat is increasing and my lungs are beginning to hurt. I don't have much time. I focus on my magic, drawing some of it into me. I can't hurt Crispin, but I will be able to make him regret this.

"Let her go," a deep voice suddenly shouts from the other side of the courtyard, the direction from where we entered. Storm. What is he doing here?

I send some icy air against Crispin's face, hoping it will make him lift his hands to protect himself. No such luck, if only, his grip tightens.

Stars are beginning to dance before my eyes and my lungs are screaming for air.

I wrap wind magic around his arms and waist, and pull, while anchoring myself in place with more magic. Nothing happens. It's as if he's not there. My magic isn't having any effect on him.

Suddenly, there's something on my throat, something real this time. Cold and sharp. A knife. Even having it on my skin hurts. This isn't a normal knife. It feels evil, wrong.

"He said, let her go."

Wait, that's Crispin speaking. How is Crispin both behind me and standing next to Storm?

I think the lack of oxygen is making me hallucinate.

"I was supposed to capture her, but I'm allowed to kill her, so stand back," the Crispin holding me warns. His voice is cold and impassionate, so unlike my Crispy.

The blackness is increasing and my legs are going limp. I'd fall to the ground if he wasn't holding me tight. Still, the movement surprises him and the knife cuts into my skin.

I'm too weak to even scream as pain races through me. Even though the wound is only on my throat, it hurts everywhere. I focus on my magic and shudder as I see black tendrils run through my veins, mixing with my blood. Something is flowing from the knife into me. I need to stop it.

Thinking is getting more and more difficult.

Stop the blackness.

I reach out to my magic and let her loose.

"Get rid of it," I tell her. "Destroy it."

She purrs and jumps up, towards the black tendrils spreading further and further through my body.

"Arc, now!" I hear from far away, but my ears are no longer working properly. Nothing is working. I can't see, I can't speak, and I definitely can't breathe.

The black magic is burning me. I need to get away from it.

I draw further into myself, cowering in the cave my magic usually resides in. I can feel her fight against the intruders, but I'm not sure if she's strong enough.

I'll wait here.

And sleep.

I need to sleep.

So tired.

"She's breathing again!"

"Finally!"

"Wyn, can you hear me?"

"Give her some space!"

I blink my eyes open, expecting darkness like earlier, but I can see again – and it's no longer night. I'm not in the gardens anymore either.

"Ehm... where am I?" I groan, very aware that it's the oldest question in the book.

"In the healing wing," Arc answers.

I'm about to say that I've seen the healing quarters and that this room doesn't look at all like it, when Arc grins and interrupts my unspoken protest.

"This is the Royal hospital room. You didn't think the Queen or any of the Gods would lie on the general ward with the common Guardians?"

"That makes sense. Why was there a second Crispin?" I point at my blond healer who's standing on my right, worry filling his eyes.

"Long story," he sighs. "Maybe you should rest first. Your wound still isn't healed completely."

"My wound?"

He points at my throat.

"Don't touch it. I put a dressing on it so it won't get infected."

I look at him in confusion. "You didn't heal me?"

He cringes. "I tried. It was a Summer blade... I couldn't do anything." His shoulders begin to shake and Frost puts an arm around his shoulders.

"Not your fault, mate. Nobody can heal wounds inflicted by that knife."

I frown. "So how am I alive and talking?"

"You healed yourself," Crispin says quietly. "Your magic fought the Summer poison. When you stopped breathing though... We thought you'd gone back to the Library, but when you didn't wake up, we knew that you hadn't. Your heart was still beating though... I didn't know what to do."

He looks so lost, so full of despair, that I stretch out a hand and pull him onto the bed. Surprised by my sudden gesture, he trips and almost falls on top of me, but Storm manages to catch him just in time before he crushes me.

"Careful, don't squash the Princess," Storm says sternly but there's a small laugh in his voice.

I laugh. "Did you just make a joke?"

He shrugs. "I do have my moments."

"Well, five stars for bedside manner," I tease and he smiles.

Crispin adjusts his position until he's lying next to me on the bed, hugging me close. I think the hug is more for him than for me, but I'm okay with that. I know how bad he must have been feeling. He's a healer, he's the most talented healer in the

Realm, and still he wasn't able to help me. For someone who's always wanting to help others, this must have been frustrating and terrifying at the same time.

"So, tell me about that other Crispin," I demand, wrapping an arm around the healer. I'm trapped beneath my blanket, otherwise I'd use my legs to draw him closer too.

"He's another creation of the Morrigan," Arc blurts out. "She made a second Crispin. Maybe more. Like clones." He shudders in disgust. "I thought she'd have more imagination than creating the same Guardian again."

"I'm prettier," Crispin grumbles next to me and I run my fingers over his smooth golden hair.

"You are," I whisper. "You're the prettiest Crispin out there."

He chuckles slightly, but there's a lot of darkness in his eyes as he looks straight at me.

"Didn't you mean Guardian?"

"What?"

"Prettiest Guardian," he clarifies. "Not just the prettiest Crispin. For all I know, there's only two of us."

"Let's hope so," Storm mutters darkly. "There could be dozens of new Crispins."

"Could we stop calling them my name?" Crispin protests, and while he laughs while saying it, it's clear that it hurts.

"Let's call them clones," I suggest. "They may look like you from the outside, but not at all on the inside. In there, you're unique." I place a hand on his chest, feeling his steady heartbeat.

"What happened to the clone who attacked me?"

"He's in the dungeons," Storm says. "We wanted to wait with interrogating him until you're awake again. He had some poison with him, just like the others, but we took it off him before he could take it."

"Good, let's go."

"Are you sure you're feeling up to it," Crispin asks, the healer in him coming to the surface. "We should do some tests…"

"I don't need tests," I interrupt him. "I want to talk to that fake Crispin who tricked me and cut my skin."

"Is the knife's magic completely destroyed?" Frost asks and I focus on my magic to make sure. She's back in her cave, sleeping peacefully, her belly round like she's just had a large meal. If she's calm like that, it means there are no more threats inside my body.

"All clear," I tell the guys. "Let's interrogate this bastard. I have a few things to say to him."

I jump out of bed, noticing that I'm in a white gown.

"Seriously? I look like you were close to putting me in a coffin."

"We cremate our dead," Arc protests but Frost interrupts him.

"Has anybody ever told you that you can be scary when you look this determined?"

"No? But that's good. I want to make that clone feel fear."

After a quick stop by my own rooms to get dressed in something less pathetic, I lead the men down into the dungeons. The last time I was here, I came to see the dragon prisoner. I wonder where he and Ada are right now. I still feel a little betrayed by the Guardian's disappearance. She's a strong warrior, we could use her in the battles to come. Maybe she'll be back, but I don't count on it. Something's going on with her and the dragons, but there's no time for us to find out.

"He's in the cell furthest to the right," Storm tells me. He's been trying to take the lead ever since we descended into the lower levels of the Palace, but I'm not letting him. It's my right to speak to the man who tried to kill me. If he is a man, not a monster.

I immediately feel bad for thinking that. Once, Crispin would have been like him. Killing for the Morrigan without second thought. Did he feel the same pleasure about it that his clone exuded? I shudder when I remember hearing the clone's voice, his warm breath on my ear. He'd been creepy. I can't believe I didn't notice immediately that it wasn't my Crispin – but then, why would I have expected a doppelganger? I didn't think that was possible.

We reach the last cell and its inhabitant. He's lying on the ground, his legs drawn to his chest. There's dried blood darkening his blond hair and bruises forming on his flawless skin.

"We never said we brought him here unharmed," Storm shrugs unapologetically.

"Is he conscious?" I ask and Crispin concentrates for a moment.

"Yes, he's just pretending to be asleep. He's in pain but nothing life-threatening."

I turn to the prisoner. "Look at me," I command loudly, putting as much authority as I can into my voice.

He laughs roughly. "No."

I grimace. "Did you know that while you can't use magic in these cells, we can use magic out here to affect you? You won't be able to defend yourself... you're at our mercy, basically."

"Then kill me and be done with it."

His voice lacks all emotion, but for some reason, it makes me shiver. He's speaking with Crispin's voice, but it's still not the same. Now that I know they're two different people, I can easily keep them apart. Crispin is full of warmth and emotion, even when he tries to hide it. This clone is cold and full of darkness.

He finally lifts his head and looks at me.

"What are you waiting for?"

I meet his gaze, refusing to look away.

"I'm not going to kill you. But you're going to answer my questions."

"And if I don't?"

"My friends here are all very talented." I point at my four guys. "One of them in particular. Arc here would love to invade your mind and pull all the information we need, right?"

The kilted Guardian smiles grimly. "With pleasure."

"Will it hurt, Arc?" I ask innocently, as if I didn't know already.

"Oh aye, it will hurt. People say it's pain like nothing else. Like your brain is sucked out through yer nose."

"And will his mind be okay afterwards?"

He shrugs. "I dinnae ken, but usually, they end up a little stupid. Drooling, helpless, whining, ..."

"Yes, I think we get the picture," I interrupt him, and turn back to the prisoner. "Now, shall we start with your name?"

"Crispin," the clone says through gritted teeth.

The real Crispin next to me growls and steps forward.

"No, you're not. That's my name, you can't have it."

The clone smiles, exposing a few missing teeth. My men must have been rougher with him than I realised. Serves him right.

"She told me about you," he says, looking straight at Crispin. "Her failed experiment. She was very disappointed with you. Such a failure. When she lost you, she was happy. She finally got rid of you and had the opportunity to make me. An improved version. I'm you as you should have been."

I put a hand on Crispin's shoulder, holding him back from reacting to the prisoner's words. They must hurt. Despite all the Morrigan did to him, I know that inside, he's still not fully healed. He's still not over the bond he had with her. He was an addict back then, addicted to her praise and approval. He would have done anything for a kind word from her. It makes my heart ache to see how he's suffering even now. We shouldn't have taken him with us, but I know we couldn't have held him back either.

"How are you improved?" I ask the clone, keeping a neutral tone as if I'm genuinely interested.

"She wanted him to feel so that he could enjoy the pain of others like she does. It backfired and he began to feel the wrong things. She decided to make me not feel at all."

I swallow hard at that revelation.

"But you're smiling. Why are you smiling when you don't feel anything?"

"It's what you expect from the bad guy, don't you," he counters. "You want me to look like I'm enjoying all the evil things I do. My Mistress thinks that makes me even scarier and therefore more effective. I can stop smiling, if you wish."

Immediately, his face goes blank, as if he's never felt an emotion in his life – now that's just creepy. Even his eyes are completely without expression.

I almost preferred if he smiled again. That makes him look slightly human at least. Now he looks like a zombie, except that he's intelligent and very dangerous.

"You said the Morrigan sent you to bring me to her. What does she want with me?"

He shrugs. "A bargaining chip perhaps? Someone new to torture? Who knows."

"He's lying," Arc whispers from behind me. "He knows exactly."

I wish I had that ability. Back on Earth, I was able to tell if humans were lying, but I can't do it with Guardians and Gods. I asked Arc to teach me, but apparently, it's not magic as such, more like a seventh sense that tells him if people are truthful or not.

"Stop lying," I tell the clone. "You've got one more chance before I give you to Arc to play with."

Arc laughs cruelly, and even though I know it's just for show – he hates using his mind powers for this purpose – it almost convinces me. The prisoner however looks at me blankly. I guess if he doesn't have any emotions, he can't feel fear either. Damn, that's going to make things more difficult.

He sits up and stretches out his arms. "Do your worst."

I sigh and step to one side to give Arc access.

"He's all yours. Try to get as much information as possible before his brain gets fried."

"Aye," Arc grumbles and approaches the bars separating us from the prisoner. "Storm, open the door and hold him in place."

I see Storm's wind magic weave tight ropes around the clone's arms and legs, fixing him in place. When he's secured, the door springs open and Arc enters the cell. Even though the fake Crispin shouldn't be able to move, I feel a twinge of fear for my Guardian. I quickly push it to one side though. Arc can handle himself.

My Scottish Guardian sits down opposite the clone and reaches forwards, putting a hand on the other man's forehead. The prisoner flinches slightly, but then his eyes roll back and his lids flutter shut.

Arc closes his eyes as well as he dives into the clone's mind, getting us the information we need. There's nothing the rest of us can do but wait.

I take Crispin's hand and he squeezes it tightly. His skin is damp and there's a slight tremor to his touch.

"You can leave now," I whisper. "We can do this without you."

He shakes his head. "No, I want to be here. I need to see this. I need to know if there are more of us."

"More of them," I correct. "You're nothing like him. You heard it, she took away all of his emotions. She saw that as your flaw, but it's your biggest strength. You wouldn't be the

Crispin I know, the helpful, considerate, loving Crispin without feeling like you do."

I reach up and press a kiss on his lips. Immediately, he wraps his arms around my waist and pulls me closer, leaning down a little to make it easier for me. Why are all my men so tall? Or is it me who's too small? Either way, kissing is easier when we're sitting or lying on the bed. But right now, there's no other option, and I wouldn't change it for the world.

His lips are soft and gentle, and I don't press him to be faster. It's a slow kiss, full of reassurance. I'm telling him that he's mine and that I love him, no matter his past and his connection to the monster behind us. In his kiss, there's all the anxiety and worry he's been feeling, and I try and take it away from him, slowly sucking it into myself, away from him. I intensify the kiss and he responds, opening his mouth a tiny bit and I playfully nudge his lips to open further. He groans, his chest vibrating against mine.

"Can you continue this later?" Frost jokes. "I think Arc is almost done."

Despite wanting to continue, I end the kiss with one last flick of my tongue against his upper lip. I turn around, but Crispin doesn't release me, simply continuing his hold on me, his hands now on my belly rather than on my back. I lean against his chest, enjoying his warmth.

It takes me a moment to find the resolve to look at the prisoner. Arc still has his hand on the man's forehead, but the clone is no longer sitting up straight. No, he's hanging in Storm's bonds, probably unconscious. His face is contorted into a grimace of pain and I almost feel sorry for him... almost.

With a deep sigh, Arc opens his eyes and removes his hand before leaning back. His forehead is covered in tiny pearls of sweat and he looks exhausted.

"What did you find out?" I ask but he shakes his head.

"Let's talk away from here. I need a wee dram."

Chapter Thirteen

It turns out that Arc doesn't just need a 'wee dram' – he ends up downing half a bottle of whisky. Once he wipes his mouth and puts the bottle back on the whisky shelf in the Palace Guards Office – I didn't know this existed until moments ago – he sighs and begins to speak.

"That bawbag really didn't feel anything. I've never been in a mind like his. It was empty and full at the same time. Like it wasn't all his own thoughts, like he was just a vessel and someone had filled it with their own ideas and commands."

"The Morrigan," I say darkly and he nods.

"Her traces were all over his mind. Her influence runs deep, much deeper than just creating him. She's fed him her lies from the moment he was created, and she's reinforced them every day. He's been like a sponge, drinking it all up, feeding off it. He dinnae feel but he has desires – the same as the Morrigan's. He wants what she wants, and he will do whatever it takes to please her. I guess he might have enough of a connection to her that he'd feel if she's happy, and that might fill the hole in him for just a bit. It's sad really, how he's her lapdog despite his obvious intelligence.

"She's got complete control of him, and I dinnae think there's a way of breaking it. If we set him free, he'll run back to her... if he can still run." His voice turns ominous. He must have wrought quite a lot of damage while extracting information from the clone's mind.

"No way are we letting him go anywhere. He stays here, even if he rots in dungeons for the rest of his life," I say, ignoring how violent that sounds. As a ruler, you sometimes have to make unpleasant decisions. And in his case, it's not even all that unpleasant. He hurt me – the cut on my throat is still throbbing – and would hurt my Guardians if he could.

"I was speaking hypothetically," Arc replies with a grim smile. "After what I've seen, I'd never let him out of my sight. He's done terrible things, Wyn. Believe me, ye don't want ta ken about most of them. And there are others like him. I'm not sure how many, but we need to be prepared to see more fake Crispins in the future. But what's important is that I've seen the Morrigan's lair."

"Please don't tell me it's Castle Tioram?" I ask and he shakes his head.

"No. Kind of. Tioram is a Gate, but one that only leads to her Realm, nowhere else."

"Wait, what? The Morrigan doesn't have a Realm. My mother expelled her and gave her lands to other Gods."

Arc shakes his head. "Sadly, that's no longer true. She's made herself a new Realm from the ruins of several zones of the Demon Realm. She started off with one zone, enslaving the demons. Then she used them to conquer more, until she ruled most of the demon lands. She knows we're monitoring the Gates leading to the Demon Realm, so she built her own."

"That's impossible," Storm interrupts. "Nobody can build Gates by themselves."

Arc sighs. "Ye can if ye sacrifice a thousand demons ta create it."

I think all of us are dumbstruck by that. I mean, I don't like demons and I killed quite a few myself. But killing a thousand of them, and probably a lot more while she conquered their Realm in the first place... wow.

"So that means Castle Tioram is just a front to prevent us from knowing that she lives in the Demon Realms?"

"Aye," Arc confirms. "And if we'd gone there tomorrow, we'd likely only seen a ruined castle. But now that we ken, we can lie in wait and enter the Gate when someone exits."

"What? No way are you entering the Demon Realm by yourselves," I protest. "That's what we have our army for. We know her weak spot now, we can send our forces to Tioram and assault her on her own territory. That's much better than waiting for her to attack us. We finally have an advantage, let's use it."

"She has hundreds of thousands of demons, Wyn. We won't stand a chance with a frontal assault. We need ta use stealth, sneak in and strike her before she knows we're there."

I frown, giving him my most disapproving stare. "I hope that 'we' refers to some of the army's scouts, not any of you four."

He has the decency to look slightly guilty.

"We are the best there are," he says without false pride. It's a statement, the truth. "If we want ta succeed, we need ta send the best."

I'm tempted to order them not to go, but I know that they really are the best.

"Not all of you though, right?" I ask, keeping my voice as steady as possible. I don't want to seem too needy. It's a simple fact though that I need them.

"I will stay here," Crispin says softly.

I know he's not just doing that to keep my company, but also because his reaction to the Morrigan might be unpredictable. Who knows what hold she still has over him. She had decades to manipulate him, and from the shadows that have been clouding his gaze recently, it's clear that he's been struggling to fight his demons.

I take his hand and he pulls me into his arms from behind, putting his hands on my stomach and his chin on my head. It's a weird kind of supporting hug, where I can take in everyone else's reaction but still get the benefit of his soothing touch.

"Her illusions are strong," Arc remarks, almost as if in awe. "I'll need ta be there to break them and shield our minds." He gives me a big smile. "Dinnae worry, Wyn, the twins and me are a good team. We'll be back before ye know it."

"Don't patronise me," I hiss, but I'm smiling to show that I don't quite mean it. Maybe I do. I don't know, my emotions are all over the place. Not long ago, I would have fought to come with them, but now I have responsibilities. I can't leave the Realm without a ruler. My mother is still in bed, too weak to even sit up on her own.

When did I become so... royal?

"You always have been," Crispin whispers into my ear.

It takes me a moment to realise that he answered a question I didn't ask out loud.

I turn and look at him in confusion. "Did you just read my mind?"

He frowns, just as confused. "No, you asked us a question."

"I certainly didn't. Did I?"

Frost shakes his head. "I didn't hear anything."

"But she spoke," Crispin insists. "She asked about when she became so royal."

"Nope, she didn't." Storm looks at us strangely. "Wyn, is your bond to us evolving?"

"I've been feeling more of your emotions through it," I admit. "Does that mean we can finally communicate through it? More than just nudges, I mean. Actual talking."

"Say something to me," Frost demands, his eyes flashing in delight.

Storm is amazing, I think.

Crispin laughs heartily, but none of the others react.

Arc frowns and steps forward, putting one hand on my shoulder.

"Try again."

What is he wearing under his kilt?

"Nothing," he replies, his gaze turning smouldering. "It must be touch. Crisp and I touch her, and we can hear what she thinks."

"Maybe that's the first step," Storm muses. "It could be that soon the bond allows us to talk over distances as well."

I huff. "Would be nice if it allowed us to do that now already. It would give us a major advantage while you're away chasing evil Goddesses."

"Ya never know. It might develop overnight," Arc says, but he doesn't sound convinced.

For now, I guess we'll just have to wait and see. Although I should be careful with what I think when I touch them. Oh my. What happens when we're in bed together? Will they all hear my thoughts as well as my moans? That would be embarrassing...

"When will you leave?" I ask the guys to change the topic and they all look at Storm.

"Arc needs to rest," he says determinedly, ignoring the Scots protests. "Then it's at least a three-hour flight to the Western Gate. Once we arrive at Calanais, provided we encounter no more demons, we'll drive to Stornoway, then take the private plane from there to somewhere near Castle Tioram – I need to check a map. If the closest airport is Oban, it'll be at least two hours to drive to the castle. In short, it will take us some time to get there, and we don't know how long we'll be in the Demon Realms. Time flows differently there; we could be gone for days."

"Maybe we should leave during the ball tonight," Frost suggests. "If the Morrigan has spies in the Palace, they'll be distracted."

"Is that long enough for Arc to recuperate?"

I'm not asking the Scot directly, because I know he'd downplay his weaknesses. But I saw how exhausted he looked after he searched through the clone's mind, and Storm is right, we need Arc at his strongest.

Before Arc can say something, Crispin steps forward and puts a hand on his arm.

"Yes," he says after a moment. "He'll be fine."

Arc pushes the healer away and rubs his arm as if Crispin left a mark on it.

"I'm fine," he grumbles. "But I concede that the ball will be a good distraction. Better get our supplies ready."

"While you do that, I should inform the Queen," I sigh. "I'm sure my mother would like to know what's happening."

"I'll come with you," Crispin announces. "I ought to check on her anyway."

Storm nods, all business. "Good. I'll choose some of our elite soldiers to accompany us to Tioram. We need to be stealthy, so not too many, but enough to have some backup."

It takes all my willpower not to protest. Am I really letting three of my guys go into danger without me? After all our adventures on Earth – and a few assassination attempts here in the Realm – I feel like they won't be safe without me, just like I won't be safe without them. Splitting up seems like a bad idea.

Beira looks like she's getting worse, not better. Her cheeks are sunken in and her eyes are only half open while she listens to me. At one point, she takes my hand, but even that movement seems too much for her.

As soon as I've updated her on what's about to happen, I leave. She didn't have anything to say, and that scares me. It either means that everything we're planning is good, or, more likely, that she didn't have the energy to come up with improvements to our plans.

Crispin stays with her, making sure that there are no ailments affecting her body in addition to the severe lack of magic. He said something about her immune system being weakened by lying in bed for so long, but I trust him to do all he can for her.

From tonight, I'll have to be worried for five people rather than my current two: Beira, my father, Storm, Frost and Arc.

Luckily, they all know what my dad looks like, so hopefully they're going to be able to bring him home. Even if they aren't able to disturb the Morrigan's plans in other ways, that alone would be success enough for me.

I push the thoughts of my father far away. I can't dwell on his fate just now. I need to be strong. As silly as it seems to throw a ball in times of war, I can see why we're doing it. Gods aren't like humans and Guardians. They're not as concerned with the affairs of others, and far more interested in their own pleasures.

Tamara told me how Beira often entertains them with pretty Guardians, letting them have some fun before she starts negotiations with them. That way, their physical tastes are already sated and they'll be happier than they were before. It makes getting what she wants easier.

I have no intention of providing prostitutes tonight though. That's really not compatible with my morals. Once again, I'm reminded that I grew up in a very different place from the Realms. Sex is far more natural here, and it's not unusual to see some of the Palace Guardians in various stages of pleasure, their bodies entwined, others openly watching. It's not that I'm prude, but it takes some time getting used to. When I meet one of my guys and we have some time... well, we usually seek out an empty room, we don't do it in the corridors. I don't think that will change either. I prefer them for myself. Others aren't allowed to see them. Not their good bits, anyway. It's okay for others to see their faces. That's kind of unavoidable.

I stop by the kitchens, getting myself a cinnamon bun for lunch. Everyone is busy preparing for tonight's feast, so I leave them be and head to my own chambers. The new ones, since I destroyed my old rooms. Through some kind of magic, they've managed to make them look almost the same. Even the clothes in my wardrobe are the same.

Not quite sure what to do, I sit down on my soft bed. Everybody else is busy, but here I am, sitting alone in my bedroom. I could go to my mother's study and look at more papers, but I might do that once my Guardians have left, to distract myself. Maybe I should talk to Flora, find out more about the Spring Realm? No, I can do that tonight, especially if I need to look busy and important. I don't want the visiting Gods to think that I'm desperate for attention. If I talk to Flora and then have to excuse myself to talk to others, it might give them the impression that I'm doing them a favour by even chatting to them. That's one thing I've learned here in the Realms: it's all about appearances.

A blue folder on the small desk in the corner catches my eye. That wasn't there before. I get up to take a look. It's a list of all the Gods going to attend tonight. Tamara must have been busy. I smile. Her neat handwriting is full of little flourishes and playful swirls, as if writing this list gave her genuine pleasure. I certainly hope so.

She's written a short commentary for each of the Gods we've invited.

Dagda – known as a Celtic creation God, but all he creates is heartbroken ladies. He's got a small but efficient army. Not much powers himself but skilled diplomat. Charm and smiles will make him interested. Flirting always works.

Vulcan - God of Fire and Metalworking. A bit rough around the edges but inside he's quite a nice fellow. Loves dark chocolate, I'll tell the servants to give him some. His hammer is smaller than Thor's, don't comment on that.

Saturn - God of Wealth. He's extremely proud, be sure to mention casually that a planet is named after him. Try not to stare at his hair... it's lush.

I quickly flick through the pages. There's at least fifty Gods to read about. Looks like I'll be busy after all.

Chapter Fourteen

The nightmare has begun. No, nothing to do with the Morrigan or Angus.

I'm having to wear a dress. A monstrosity. Tight, frilly, far too large a neckline. My boobs are practically falling out of it, held back only by a small band of lace.

Why do Gods have such a terrible fashion sense? They're all about showing as much skin as possible while also showing wealth and importance with the quality of the fabrics.

Tamara is giggling loudly while I inspect myself in the mirror.

"I'm going to flash Gods," I mutter, trying to adjust the inbuilt – but almost non-existent – bra.

"It will help, they'll like that," Tamara snorts and I shoot her an evil look. I'm tempted to give her the finger as well, but I've learned they don't have that gesture here in the Realm.

"I don't like it though," I protest.

"She's not going to show our boobs to them."

I whirl around and gape at Frost who's entered the room without me noticing.

"Did you just say 'our boobs'?" I'm kind of speechless.

"Of course. You're ours, so they're our boobs. And others don't get to see them. Our Wyn, our boobs."

Tamara snickers. "I'll leave you two to it. Ball starts in half an hour, don't take too long."

With a knowing wink, she leaves and closes the door behind her.

"They're my boobs," I challenge Frost. "They're attached to my body. You can't have them."

"Oh, I can't?" He slowly stalks towards me, his eyes fixed on my chest. "Are you sure?"

Heat is flushing through my body as his words take full effect. His sultry voice isn't helping, neither is the fire burning in his eyes.

I swallow and square my shoulders. This is going to be fun.

"I think you need to prove it," I challenge him.

"With pleasure," he whispers huskily and a moment later, he pushes me without warning and I land on my back on the bed. My arms stretch to both sides as I try to cushion the fall – not that it's needed with a mattress this soft – and the fabric of the dress rips.

I lift my head to stare at the damage.

Fuck.

The lace is gone and my breasts are now fully exposed.

Frost is laughing heavily and I glare at him – and at the dress. Who came up with this provocative design? And who made it rippable?

I pull up some of the fabric from below, but it's too tight around my chest and doesn't budge at all.

"Don't move, I want to enjoy the view," Frost tells me, his voice filled with both laughter and desire.

Resigned to my fate – and very much looking forward to it – I lean back again, my arms outstretched, my boobs in full view.

Frost stalks towards the bed and climbs on the mattress, his knees on either side of me. He looks like he's about to devour me whole. I shiver and pleasant tingles run all over my skin.

"Don't move," he whispers, but it's not necessary. I have no intention to change my position. The way I'm exposed to him, unable to hide my naked skin, is exhilarating. He's not even touching me, but I can feel the heat of his gaze as much as if his hands were running over my skin. The connection between us is vibrating somehow, as if the bond is telling us that it's still there. Thanks, I didn't need that reminder. I'm very aware of how close Frost is, of how he looks at me, of how he's reaching out and...

I arch my back as his fingers touch my skin.

He chuckles in surprise. "I don't think I've ever had that effect on a woman before."

Trust me, I've not behaved like this before. Usually I need someone to touch me before I let go of my inhibitions like that. But right now, it's different. I want him so much.

I sink back to the bed and promise myself I won't react like –

He touches my skin again and I moan loudly. I can't help it. It's like his touch his enhanced a thousand-fold and my senses are telling me that he's touching me in other places, between my legs, on my lips, but I know he's not. He only has two fingers on my right breast, twirling my nipple between them.

"What's going on?" I gasp as he begins to touch my other boob.

"I'm not sure, but I feel it too," he whispers and nods towards his crotch. I lift my head and look down. He's straining against his trousers, ready to be let out to play.

"Fuck me," I moan. "Stop the foreplay. Just do it. I need it now."

He nods sharply and leans back to take off his trousers. I moan again as soon as he stops touching me. I need more.

I don't need to wait long though. He ruffles up the skirt of my dress and pulls it up. He doesn't bother to pull down my panties, he simply rips them apart. Wow. Has he ever done that before? My thoughts are too heated to remember.

Then he's within me, his cock hard and satisfying, pressing against my core, his hands on my breasts, his lips on my throat, his essence entwined with mine. We're one, together.

I meet his lips, kissing him deeply, drowning in all the emotions he's throwing at me. I can feel parts of him I've never felt before. Dreams... memories... thoughts...

He groans loudly and with a final thrust of his hips, he comes in me, and I around him, squeezing him tight with my thighs, my back arched against the mattress, riding the waves that press us together even more.

Something makes me close my eyes and suddenly I can see myself. What? It's me, lying on the bed, my hair dishevelled, the dress bunched up around my belly. I look down and see my cock-

I open my eyes and sit up with a flash, shaking my head widely to get that image out of my mind.

"What the fuck..." Frost mutters, looking at me strangely. "Is that what I look like?"

"What? My cock..." I stammer, not sure how to form coherent sentences. "You..."

"Heh?"

"I was in your head."

"And I in yours." He looks just as confused as I feel. "I need to shave."

I start laughing hysterically. "That's the first thing you think of? You're so vain."

He steps back, a frown ruining his perfect face. "What just happened? How did that happen? Why...?"

I shake my head, sitting up and readjusting my dress until I'm slightly less exposed. Down below, at least, nothing I can do about my boobs hanging out.

"I have no idea. That was strange. The whole thing. How long did it take? Like, a minute for both of us to come? I mean, I love you and want you, but that was fast, out of nowhere..."

I stop speaking. There's nothing more to be said. He knows exactly what happened. He felt it too. Hell, he saw through my eyes just like I saw through his.

"Has this ever happened with any of the others?" he asks.

I smile grimly. "Don't you think I would have told you?"

"Yeah, you're right. Is it the bond? You've said it's become more intense, and Crispin heard your thoughts earlier... but it's changing fast."

"Maybe. It's been getting stronger slowly, very slowly, but suddenly this is all happening so quick. Maybe it's because you're leaving? Maybe it knows that?"

"Are we talking about the bond as if it's sentient?" he asks, but I just shrug. Maybe we are. It's a weird thing, that bond. Especially because it isn't just one. The first bond was formed when they took some of my magic into themselves, back during my first flare. Then the second we formed on purpose with a ritual. Maybe they're combining into something stronger?

I get up from the bed and take off the ruined dress. With my back to him, I ask, "Do you think it will happen again?"

"Having sex with you? I sure hope so."

I laugh. "You know what I mean."

"It would be strange for it to be a one-off," he says, more serious this time. "But I hope it won't all be this rushed next time."

"Yeah, me too," I mutter as I step into a new dress, this one a lot less extravagant this time. No more frilly stuff. It's sleek, simple, and Tamara is going to tell me off for wearing it. "Can you zip me up?"

Frost steps behind me and wraps his arms around my waist, not at all doing what I asked him to. He nuzzles my neck with his lips, his hot breath doing things to my stomach that I want to feel a lot more of. How insatiable am I today? I need to meet some Gods in a few minutes and here I am, turning into a needy, hormonal woman at the simple touch of a Guardian.

My Guardian.

"Stop it," I whisper half-heartedly, the responsible Princess in my fighting for dominance. I ignore her. She can come out when I'm talking to the Gods, not now.

Rather than zipping up the dress, Frost pushes it down my shoulders until I'm half-naked again. I don't protest. Nope. I can always blame him if I'm late for the party.

His lips draw a line on my neck, slowly moving towards my right shoulder. He's mixing his kisses with tiny bites, each of them sending lightning bolts straight into my core. He shouldn't be allowed to do stuff like that. It makes me all weak and moany.

I can feel him hard against my back; he doesn't seem to have put his trousers back on. I'm sure we still have time for another quick-

I'm back in his head, looking at the smooth skin in front of me. I run a finger over her collarbone, admiring how perfectly it curves. She's so beautiful, so stunning. I want to keep her here with me, never let her go. My brothers can join us, but nobody else. Just the five of us, locked into this room. Let the world go to-

I gasp, back in my own body. The dress slips down my body as Frost steps back. I immediately miss his touch. My cheeks heat at the thought of what I just saw. Of what he was thinking. I never knew he was this possessive.

"Were you...?" I ask and turn around, pretty sure the same just happened to him.

"I like your mind," he says simply. "It's so pure."

I laugh. "You must have been in someone else's head. My mind is the opposite of pure. And I have to say, I like what you were thinking."

That's when I notice I'm half-naked, he's half-naked, and of course someone takes that exact moment to knock on the door.

"Princess, it's time!" Tamara calls from the other side of the door. "Do you need help with your hair?"

I look into the mirror and take in my dishevelled look and flushed skin. I think there's not much that can be done to make me presentable. At least I'll be able to put on a different wig and have the perfect hairstyle within seconds.

"Five minutes!" I shout back and pull up my dress, turning around so Frost can zip me up. Maybe we'll manage it this time without kisses and our hormones going wild.

As if.

Chapter Fifteen

Gods like to party.

I don't.

Not like this, anyway. Not when I have to shake hands, exchange pleasantries with Gods I've never met and people bowing in front of me. My idea of a party is a gettogether in a pub with some friends. Not this.

A lot more Gods than expected have come.

"They want to see the Demigoddess," Tamara whispers as she accompanies me on the way to the dais. "You were famous as soon as you were born. Now that you've returned to our world, they're curious. Demigods are known for their powers and unpredictability. Half of them probably want to see you explode during the party while the other half are interested in matchmaking."

I stop in my tracks and gape at her. "Matchmaking? Like... relationships?"

Tamara nods. "They assume that being with Beira's daughter will give them influence and power."

I shudder in disgust. "I'd rather explode and take them all with me into the abyss."

She chuckles. "I wouldn't have expected anything else from you. But please keep the exploding to a minimum. This is an important evening and we can't afford to end up with dead Gods."

I grimace. She's right, sadly. We need their support.

When we reach the dais, I turn around and look at the assembled crowd. There must be at least fifty Gods and Goddesses, maybe more. All of them are wearing their finest clothes – or maybe not, who knows if they ever put on leisurely outfits. I can't imagine Gods like Zeus in jeans. Not that he's here. He's one of the minor Gods, actually, and not worth our time. According to Tamara, he doesn't even have his own Realm. No idea how he got so famous.

Tamara gives one of the servants the signal to blow a trumpet. Yes, an actual trumpet. It's strange how medieval some things are here. They could have just clinked some glasses together or used their magic to get everyone's attention.

Everybody falls quiet and looks up at me. My mind goes blank for a moment. What was I going to say?

"Her Royal Highness, Daughter of Winter, the Slayer of Demons, the Heir to the Throne, the Lady Wynter."

I huff in annoyance. I've told the herald several times to leave out the demon slayer bit. I'm sure most Guardians and even Gods in this room have killed demons before. It's nothing special.

I raise my voice and smile at the crowd.

"Welcome to the Winter Realm. I'm so pleased you've all managed to come at such short notice. You all know what situation is facing the Realms, and I'm sure I'm going to have some enlightening conversations with many of you tonight. But for now, please enjoy the food and entertainment. I know many of you are curious about the place I grew up in, so I have personally chosen some Earth delicacies for you to try."

No, I haven't, that was all Arc's idea. He told the cooks to make some British nibbles like sausage rolls and puff pastry pies. He then decided to add some fried haggis balls to the menu. The whisky sauce has mysteriously disappeared though, and I wonder if it's ended up in Arc's enormous stomach. I hope he and the others know not to get drunk tonight. They have an evil Goddess's Realm to infiltrate.

Food appears on the long tables and the Gods take their places. There are Guardians among them as well, probably servants, assistants, protectors, lovers, that kind of thing.

I turn to Crispin, who's taken a seat next to me.

"Maybe you and the others should start some conversations with the other Guardians. They might be willing to give out some information about their Gods."

He nods. "Good idea. I'll let the others know. They're all prepared, by the way. Just let them know when you think is a good time for them to leave. We should make sure that they're seen first though, just in case there are spies."

"Yes, definitely. Where are they?"

"Right behind you," Storm's deep voice says. I turn and there they are, my other three Guardians, standing behind me, their arms crossed protectively.

"Please, can you look a little less intimidating?" I ask him, although I kind of like the stern look on him. "You're supposed to mingle with the crowds and be friendly, not look like you're about to rip off heads."

"I hate mingling," Arc complains. "People cannae understand my accent."

"Stop the excuses. Your accent is charming. Use it on the ladies."

It hurts a little to say that. I don't want him talking to other women. I want him all for myself. But this is politics, and important. If he can charm a female Guardian to divulge secrets about her God to him, then it's worth the pangs of jealousy in my chest.

"What we really need to know is who is willing to support us when the worst happens. Who will stand against us. And who won't get involved at all. Then we need to know about their forces. How strong are their armies? How strong is their magic? Will they be assets or not worth our trouble?"

They already know all that but I'm repeating it for my own sake as well. If I'm going to suffer in a dress amongst posh and dramatic Gods, then it needs to have a good reason.

"Spoken like a true monarch," Crispin whispers approvingly. "Now eat something, you don't want to look like you're scheming."

I look down at the plate that's appeared before me. It has some of my favourite dishes on it, both from the Realm and from Earth. I'm too nervous to eat much, but I get Crispin's reasoning. I need to pretend to enjoy this, even though I could think of a thousand places I'd rather be.

While my father is rotting in the Morrigan's dungeon, I'm throwing a ball. How pathetic.

I nibble on a piece of Yorkshire pudding – it's delicious – and watch the Gods and Goddesses below. Some are completely focussed on their food, shovelling it into their mouths, others are talking to each other, while others still are fondling their Guardians. I turn away in embarrassment. It's a different world for sure.

This kind of hedonism really isn't for me. I wish Beira was here with me to take away some of the pressure, but she's in bed, sleeping. Crispin checked on her just before he came here and told me that there's been no change in her condition. I'm not sure if that's good or bad.

Someone is approaching the dais, a very blond, no, very golden God. His hair is like pure shimmery gold, as is his skin, and his robes. I've never seen anyone so radiant. His face looks strangely chiselled, without any smooth lines at all.

When he's reached my table, he lifts his head, showing me his amber eyes. There are golden swirls in them, beautiful and hypnotising.

"Apollo," Crispin whispers into my ear.

My eyes widen. Finally, a God I've heard of. He's as stunning as I would have expected. I think back to the Apollo statues I've seen on Earth. There, he usually wears a laurel crown, but not here. Yet another human invention, or does he only wear that for special occasions?

He gives me a short bow, more of a nod of his head rather than a full genuflect.

"My lady, it's a pleasure to meet you."

I get up, not wanting to have to look up to him.

"The pleasure is mine. You're famous, even on Earth. I grew up with stories about you, so I'll be interested to see how many of them are real."

I was intending to flatter him, but the last sentence came out a little wrong. Like I'm doubting the stories about him. Which I am, but he doesn't need to know that. I'm disillusioned about all the legends I heard on Earth. Only a tiny percentage of them are true, and more often than not, the Gods are the opposite of what I thought they'd be.

Apollo chuckles. "I always enjoy hearing stories about me. I have several Guardians based on Earth to supply me with the latest rumours. There aren't as many of them now as there were two thousand years ago, of course, but they're still rather entertaining."

He gives me a wide smile and I decide that he might be a good person... ehm, God... to get to know.

"I'll go mingle," Crispin says quietly and gets up, leaving his place empty for Apollo to take.

The God doesn't wait for me to invite him to sit down next to me. A strong scent of vanilla and elderflowers fills my nose when he takes his place. It's an alluring smell and I instinctively lean closer to him.

"Thanks for coming," I tell him, my mind going blank once again. "Did you have to travel far?"

He laughs as if I made the joke of the century.

"Are you seriously making small talk with the God of Poetry?"

I frown, somewhat irritated by his response.

"Poetry? I thought it was knowledge and light."

"Yes, that too," he says dismissively. "And music, art, archery, take your pick. I'm quite talented, in more ways than one."

He raises an eyebrow suggestively.

And so it begins... I had hoped there wouldn't be any flirting, but it seems these hopes were just destroyed by a God as bright as sunlight.

"That's good to know," I say, keeping my voice level. "Are you good in a fight as well?"

He roars with laughter. "Straight to the point, I see. Giving up on the small talk?"

I grin. "Why would I bore someone so talented with useless chatter. And if you're really the God of knowledge, you'll be aware of what's at stake."

He turns serious immediately. "I do indeed. Your Realm isn't the only one affected. My guards caught three parties of demon spies this week alone. I'm sure more are slipping through unseen. I hear you have a theory of who is controlling the demons?"

It's obvious that he knows already.

"It's not a theory. We know for certain that the Morrigan is in charge of the demons. She took over their Realm, effectively enslaving them."

"The Morrigan, eh? Do you have any proof? She's been gone for a long time now. What reason does she have to control demons?"

I'm not quite sure what to make of Apollo. First it seemed like he understood the problem. Now he's asking obvious questions like he's doubting me.

"Revenge. My mother took everything from her. It seems she's done lurking in the shadows and is out to show how powerful she still is."

"Only Beira and Angus are more powerful than her," Apollo says in a low voice. "If she controls the demons... you don't have much of a chance against her."

"Well, we're not going to just sit here and wait for her to invade our Realm," I reply sharply. "She may be strong, but we're not alone. We have allies, and now that she's started killing Gods, more are joining us every day."

That's a bluff, of course. The only one who's joined us recently is Flora. The Goddess of Spring is sitting on one of the tables at the other end of the hall, animatedly talking to another Goddess who's dressed in an elaborate green dress decorated with real flowers and vines. Some nature deity, perhaps?

"She's killed Gods?" Apollo raises his eyebrows, visibly surprised. I guess that news hasn't spread yet. Maybe we should make sure that everybody here knows that Fav was killed. In fact, I'll do exactly that.

"She has indeed," I tell him and get up, banging my fork against my wine glass to get the attention of our guests.

"I apologise for interrupting your dinner, but I realised you may not know the tragedy that has befallen one of our guests tonight. I would like to invite you all to stand and have a minute of silence for Favonius, who was brutally killed by the Morrigan just days ago. His widow, Flora, is here with us, and

I'm sure you'll all join me in declaring her my sincere condolences."

The hall falls quiet. Shock shows on most of the guests' faces, and some of them are beginning to whisper to each other.

"Do you have proof?" a burly God suddenly shouts, his large red beard hiding most of his face.

Flora gets up, her pale lips trembling slightly. She reaches into the tight corset hugging her delicate figure and produces a raven feather that she's been wearing between her breasts.

"One of my messengers saw her meet with Angus," she says shakily, but her voice steadies when she grips the feather more tightly, holding it up for all to see. "She tried to poison me, but my husband ate what was intended for me, and died. This feather was left on his chest, a clear calling sign of the Morrigan. She killed a God to stop the information from getting out. Angus is working with her, and together, they won't stop until they rule all the Realms. The God of Summer has long been wanting to upset the balance, but you all remember what happened the last time. Winter and Summer need to be equal, or we'll all feel the effects." She takes a deep breath, clearly audible in the silent hall.

"The Morrigan doesn't care about the balance. All she wants is power. Once she's conquered this Realm, she might even challenge Angus until she rules the Winter and Summer Realms. Imagine what that would mean for all of us. Nobody would be safe."

She raises the feather even higher. "We all need to stick together to fight her and drive her off for good. I have pledged to assist Queen Beira and her daughter. Will you do the same?"

She stands for a moment, looking around the assembled Gods. Then, with a flourish of her dress, she sits down.

Did she just do my job for me?

Before they have chance to start talking again, I shout, "A minute of silence please, for Favonius."

With a rumble of chairs, some of the Gods get up, including the one with the red beard who challenged me earlier. He holds up his large tankard and roars, "For Favonius!"

Others join his call, before falling silent. I can't believe this is happening. The mood has turned and it seems that Flora's story has moved them more than I would have been able to. The Morrigan killed one of their own, and if she did that, they probably think that they could be next.

"Thank you," I say when the minute of silence is over. "As Flora said, we need to stick together in these times of trouble. Please come and talk to me if you have questions about how we can assist each other."

I sit down and so does everyone else. It's quieter now than before, with people talking to each other rather than shouting across the hall.

We had planned to get the orchestra to play after dinner, but I tell Tamara to wait with that. We don't want the Gods to stop discussing the situation. That's what they're here for, after all.

Not far from Flora, Storm is standing with a group of Guardians, discussing something with a lot of gestures and nods. They're all listening to him; I guess that's a good sign.

I search for my other Guardians. Crispin is chatting with a dark-haired Goddess who's at least a head taller than him. She reminds me of an Amazon, with her ebony skin and her lithe figure. A warrior Goddess, perhaps?

Frost and Arc are sitting in a corner with a group of female Guardians. Figures that they'd attract the ladies. Hopefully they'll get some information out of this, not just flirting.

"Well played," Apollo says suddenly, his voice cheery. I almost forgot that he was sitting next to me.

"This isn't a game," I reply a little too harshly. Well, excuse me, my father is a prisoner, my mother ill in bed, my Guardians about to leave on a dangerous mission.

"Everything is a game," Apollo smiles. "The Morrigan has set the board and made her first moves, now it's our turn to play. By the end of tonight, you should know who is joining us on our side of the board."

"Our side?" I raise my eyebrows questioningly.

"Of course. Haven't you figured it out yet? I'm the God of Knowledge, I know a good cause when I see one."

He gets up and gives me another bow, a real one this time.

"Send my regards to your mother. I will be ready to assist should the need arise."

I'm too stunned to reply, but he's already walking away, down the dais and back to where he was sitting before. He takes a seat between two Gods, both of them dressed in earthy colours, their clothes a lot simpler than most of the others. I wonder who they are. One of them has an Asian look to him, but of course there's no Asia in the Realms.

"Well done," Tamara says from my other side. "I'll add him to our list of supporters. Hopefully, others will join him before the night is over."

Chapter Sixteen

"Stay safe," I order them, making sure they know that it's a command. They'll have to obey it. Getting hurt isn't allowed.

"Of course. We'll be back before you know it," Frost reassures me and takes me into his arms. I melt into his hug, breathing in his sea breeze scent.

Arc hugs me from behind, sandwiching me between the two Guardians. His embrace is hard and rough, like he doesn't want to let me go.

"Brother, my turn."

With a sigh, Frost steps back, letting Storm take his place. I fling my arms around his back and before I know it, his lips are on mine, kissing me hard, but just for a moment, then he's gone, as is Arc. I feel terribly alone without their touch. The echo of their warmth is still on my skin, but I want nothing more than reach out and never let them go.

"Don't die," Storm tells me gruffly.

„Don't you die either," I retort. "And bring back my father. And the Morrigan's head, if you get the chance."

"Aye, with pleasure," Arc growls. "I'll send Thomas a message as soon as we've reached Castle Tioram."

Thomas is one of the Guardians with the same mental magic Arc possesses. They can communicate over distances, even though it gets harder for them if they're not in the same Realm.

"I'll let the guards know that he's to be let into my chambers at all times."

"Not into your bedroom," Storm protests. "That's ours."

I sigh dramatically. "Please don't start the her-boobs-are-ours debate."

Arc and Storm look at me in confusion while Frost starts laughing.

"You've not told them yet?" I ask him incredulously and he shakes his head, still chuckling.

"I will on the flight."

"Looking forward ta it," Arc grins. "I like boobs."

I give them all one last hug, then usher them out of the room.

"Stay safe," I repeat. "See you soon."

The party is still in full swing when I return to the hall. The orchestra has started playing and some of the Gods are dancing, but most are still sitting in small groups, talking. I hope they're all debating whether to join us. According to Tamara, now that we have Flora and Apollo on board, we have more allies than Angus – but he has the Morrigan, who's as powerful as several Gods put together, and who has an entire demon army.

Flora comes up to me when she sees that I've returned.

"Anubis, Demeter, Krishna and Hathor have all pledged to support us. Ganesha is close, I think. Poseidon is almost convinced as well."

"Well done. Thank you for your speech earlier, it was exactly what we needed."

She shrugs. "It was the truth. They needed to know what that bitch is capable of. She's unpredictable, and who knows who she'll target next if she suspects them of knowing things they shouldn't."

"Still, thank you."

I give her a spontaneous hug and after a moment of surprise, she returns it. Her gown is smooth and silky and I'm almost jealous of it. It's strange hugging a woman – I haven't done that for a while. My mother isn't really the hugging type.

"I better get back, there were more people wanting to talk to me. Oh, and you should have a chat with Hades. He seemed interested in meeting you."

I swallow hard. I've met Hades before, although I bolted as soon as I saw him, pretending to be busy. He emanated darkness and with his reputation, I didn't feel like getting to know him closer. My mother told me off for reacting like that – Hades isn't all that bad, apparently. Like so many Gods, he's got a bad reputation, but he's not actually evil.

I better do this now before I decide otherwise.

"Thank you, Flora. I'll go look for him. If you see Crispin, can you let him know I want to talk to him?"

Hades's eyes are like bottomless pits, drawing me into their darkness. His black hair is pulled back into a ponytail, his thick brows furrowed as he looks at me. He's been doing that for half a minute now, simply observing me like some kind of specimen he's trying to figure out.

"My sister tells me she supports you," he finally says in an incredibly deep voice.

"Your sister?" I curse myself for not knowing how all the Gods here are connected. I read Tamara's notes on their abilities and powers, but most of them didn't mention if any of them were related.

"Demeter. The Goddess of the Harvest. She's been talking to Flora all evening."

He points towards a beautiful woman in a green dress, the same one I saw Flora with earlier. The vines around her waist are actually moving, gently hugging her.

How is the God of the Underworld related to a fertility Goddess? That doesn't make any sense. Maybe they're adopted? But then, that doesn't make any sense either. The Gods were created by Angus and Beira, there are no other relationship bonds. Maybe they were made at the same time and that makes them siblings?

"I've not met her yet," I admit. "But I'd love to make her acquaintance."

Hades frowns. "Trust me, you don't. She talks too much. But she's also naïve. I don't want her to get into trouble. If she fights with you, I will be there too, protecting her. I'm not your ally. I'm hers."

With that, he turns around, breaking the gaze that held me prisoner for the entire duration of our short conversation.

What a strange God. Well, I don't mind that we're not officially allies as long as he's not on Angus's side.

I make a mental note to have Tamara add him to her list of supporters.

"Godspawn, there you are!"

A roaring voice makes me turn around and almost bump into Thor. The God of Thunder isn't shirtless this time, but his leather vest doesn't leave much to the imagination. Next to him is a girl with hair just as fiery as Thor's. She's in her late teens perhaps, but while her sparkling green eyes make her seem older, an abundance of freckles on her cheeks and nose counteract that effect. She reminds me a lot of Pippi Longstocking, not just because of her name.

I notice she has a slight squint as she fixes her gaze on me curiously.

"Meet Pippa, my daughter." Thor booms, pushing the girl forwards.

She gives me an elegant courtesy, obviously used to life at Royal courts.

"Your Highness. Lovely to meet you."

I can't quite place her accent. It isn't the same Nordic sounding harshness that her father has, but a softer version of it. She smiles at me widely and I can't help but return her smile.

"Pleasure. Your father has told me a lot about you."

She sighs. "He does that a lot. I wish he'd stop telling everyone about me. It's hard to be a mysterious warrior if everybody knows who you are."

I can't hide a grin. "You're a warrior?"

"I know I don't look it but that's part of my strength," she says confidently. "People don't expect me to kick their arses."

"That's my daughter, always good for a surprise," Thor grins proudly. "She's one of the best fighters in my Realm."

"Even though you don't have magic?" I ask and instantly regret it as her face turns clouds in annoyance.

"Yes, even without magic. I don't need magic. I'm strong without it. Just because I'm human doesn't mean I'm weak."

I hold up my hands and give her a reassuring smile. "Hey, I grew up around humans, I know how strong and resilient they can be. Trust me, some of them are worth a lot more than Gods."

Her smile returns. "I wouldn't know. I've never met another human."

"Which is why I want her to spend some time on Earth," her father barges in. "Godspawn, please tell her that's a good idea."

"Only if you stop calling me that," I reply, although I quite like having a nickname. I mean, how often does it happen that the God of Thunder gives you a nickname?

He grins. "Your Royal Highness, Slayer of Demons, please tell my daughter to go to Earth."

Pippa elbows Thor in the stomach. She doesn't reach much higher, he's too tall.

"Stop it, dad. I've told you I'm not going and that's it. I don't need humans. The Realms are my home and I'd much rather visit other Realms than Earth. It sounds like a boring place."

"You're not going travelling while this war is going on," he booms, giving her a stern look. "If you want to travel, go to Earth. That's safe."

I refrain from telling him that even on Earth, there is danger. You don't need magic to hurt someone. I think humans might be less nice to each other than Gods. Here in the Realms where everyone is immortal, they need to think ahead. If they quarrel with someone, it might have implications for centuries to come. Humans don't think like that.

"Dad, can we stop this? I'm sure Wynter is terribly busy."

Pippa is giving me a pained look, as if she's had this discussion far too often. I decide to rescue her.

"Actually, she's right, I need to talk to Epona and just saw her head to the dais. Better catch her now before she thinks I'm not wanting to talk to her."

"See you later, Godspawn," Thor chuckles. "Let me know if you want another lesson."

I give them both a nod and head towards Epona. Not that I'm really as desperate to talk to the Celtic Goddess of Horses as I pretended to be, but she is on my list of Gods I want to meet.

She's a large woman wearing a leather outfit that makes her look like she's ready for battle already. Definitely not something I'd wear to a party. Her long hair is braided and wound around her head like a crown. Her nose is slightly upturned, giving her an aloof look, but her eyes are kind as she comes towards me.

She bows rather than curtsies, again separating her from the other female deities I've met today.

"My Lady. A word, if you please?"

Straight to the point, no small talk. I like it.

I nod towards the abandoned dais. Everybody has left; Crispin is mingling, my Guardians are on their way to the Western Gate, and Tamara must be busy tallying up the Gods on our side.

I pull two chairs away from the table and the tempting desserts still waiting there for my attention and take a seat, inviting Epona to do the same.

"I'm a Goddess of War," she begins without preamble. "Not like the Morrigan. I fight for a reason, not for the sake of killing. I don't sacrifice my people for purposes I don't believe in. I have created and trained every Guardian in my Realm myself, they're the best of the best. If they are to fight for you, I need to know that there is a point to this conflict."

I'm a bit confused. Flora gave all the reasons for why we fight earlier. Was Epona absent during that speech?

As if she can read my thoughts, she adds, "I want to hear it from you, Princess. If I'm fighting under your banner, I want you to be the one to tell me why I send my warriors into battle."

I nod. I get it. She's committed to the safety of her people, and that's admirable. I don't think all the Gods in here take as much care of their Guardians as Epona seems to do. If she really trains them all herself, they must be a formidable force.

"My mother is weakened," I say, not wanting to hide the truth. "With the Morrigan's help, Angus is stronger than ever before. Without help from our allies, they'd easily be able to invade the Winter Realm. The Morrigan would take over and rule this Realm, disrupting the delicate balance. All our magic depends on the balance. If it gets destroyed, the magic will malfunction. Nobody knows what effect that could have."

"Those are noble reasons," Epona replies. "But they aren't reasons my people would fight for. Give me something to believe in."

I think for a moment. What makes me hate the Morrigan the most? Why do I despise Angus?

"The Morrigan killed my adoptive mum," I say quietly. "She tortured my boyfriend. My father is still in her clutches. They tried to assassinate me and my mother. Both the Morrigan and Angus have attacked my family, and I'm not going to rest until I've punished them for it. I'm going to avenge my mum and make sure that they'll never hurt anyone ever again."

Epona looks at me for a moment and I'm almost at the point of wondering whether she'll get up and leave, when she stretches out a hand for me to shake.

"You'll have my support, Princess. Let's make the Morrigan suffer like she has made you suffer."

Her grip is firm and strong; there's a lot of power in her touch. She'll be a valuable ally.

"Thank you, Epona. I will do what I can to keep your people safe."

"I know you will." She gets up and smiles. "Once all this is over, please come and visit my Realm. I think you'd like it there. It's a little less formal than this place."

That sounds good. A holiday with my Guardians... I think I've earned that. Once we've beaten the Morrigan. First things first.

Chapter Seventeen

It's strange to only have Crispin in my bed. Usually, there's at least three Guardians sleeping with me, or four, if none of them has to do guard duties overnight. Tonight, Crispin is the only one touching me, his arms around my waist, his chest pressed against my shoulder. He's sleeping deeply, his breath slow and regular.

I'm exhausted, but sleep isn't coming. I wonder where the others are now. Have they reached the Gate yet?

I look at my watch. Four hours since they left. They should be on Earth by now. Another few hours and they'll reach Castle Tioram. Hopefully they'll be able to step through the Gate there without having to fight. Although that's a feeble hope; I'm sure there's demons guarding the entrance to their Realm.

For a moment, I remember Chesca. Without her, we wouldn't know that the Morrigan has taken over the Demon Realm. She died at the hands of one of our guards, and I still feel bad for that. I couldn't have prevented it; for them, she was just another demon. I can't really blame them. They were doing

"

their job, protecting our borders. At least she managed to get her message across before she died. As much as I despise demons, I can't help but feel like they don't deserve being ruled by the Morrigan. There must be good ones among them, like Chesca, like some of the demons she and Aodh rehabilitated. If she was still alive, she might have been able to infiltrate the Demon Realm and spy for us. But it's too late now. She's dead, buried close to the Gate where she was killed.

When I arrived here a few weeks ago, I never could have imagined I'd be fighting in a war soon after. Or that my mother would be lying in her bed, completely without magic, without her usual strength. Or that my mum would be dead.

When did life become so crazy?

Suddenly, light flashes in front of my eyes and I'm thrown into Frost's head. I know immediately that it's him; it *feels* like him.

He's standing in front of a ruined castle. The morning light is only just beginning to shine through the trees surrounding the loch the castle island is surrounded by. It's an imposing structure, even though it's got no roof and some of the walls have crumbled significantly.

A thin causeway spreads out before my men, leading towards the castle. They must have timed their arrival well because the tide is out, allowing them easy access to the little island.

How are they here already? It should have taken them longer... but I remember now, time flows slightly different on Earth than it does here. They may have already been in Scotland for hours.

As quickly as I was thrown into Frost's head, I'm out again and back in my bed. What was the point of that? Well, I guess I know now that they got there okay, but Arc was going to let his contact know anyway. Hopefully, this isn't the last time I get to see through Frost's eyes.

Wait... when this happened before, he was in my head while I was in his. Does that mean he felt Crispin pressed against him? I smile. Poor Frost. But then a darker thought grips my mind. If he's in my mind, is he defenceless in his own body? Gods, I hope not.

I don't know why these weird mind swaps are happening, and how to control them. They can't happen in battle, I won't let them. Somehow. Maybe if I strengthen my mental barriers that will prevent them from happening? As much as I want to see what Frost and the others are up to, it's not worth risking Frost's life.

I don't know when I fell asleep, but I didn't get enough of it. I rub my eyes, yawning loudly.

"You're cute when you're tired," Crispin chuckles. If I wasn't so exhausted, I'd throw a pillow at him. Instead, I just snuggle against his warm body and pretend to be still asleep. I'm ignoring the fact that Tamara is in the room, and that she just woke me.

"Your Guardians have reached Castle Tioram," she tells us, and I groan. Her voice is too loud. I want to sleep.

Mornings are evil.

"I know," I mutter into my pillow.

"How?" Crispin asks in confusion.

"Bond."

"You can talk through your bond to the others now?" he asks and I realise I haven't told him yet what happened between me and Frost.

"No."

"Are you only going to answer with one word from now on?"

"Yes."

Tamara laughs softly. "I'll leave you two to it. Council meeting is in half an hour."

I groan again, cursing life and sleep and tiredness and everything.

What did I do to deserve this?

Oh yes, I was born to a Goddess and a Guardian. Stupid genes.

Crispin gently kisses me on the forehead, running his hands over my shaved scalp.

"Lips," I grumble and he laughs, his chest vibrating against mine.

He does as I ask and the morning begins to look up a little.

It's strange not to have Magnus in attendance. In his place there's a blond-haired Guardian with stubble covering his chin and puffy cheeks, looking excited. Oh my, I hope he's up to the job. We can't afford having to train a replacement for our Treasurer now. Maybe it wasn't such a good idea to dismiss Magnus after all – but no, he was a liability. Some fresh thinking will help the Council.

"My name is Anthony, Your Highness," he introduces himself enthusiastically. "It's a pleasure to have the chance to serve you and the Realm."

Gwain is rolling his eyes at the young man's enthusiasm, but luckily, Anthony doesn't seem to notice.

"Welcome to the Council, Anthony. It's good to have you join us. Have you been able to catch up on Magnus's tasks."

"Yes, my Lady, I mean, Your Highness. I was already doing a lot of those tasks anyway, so it's not much of a change."

To be honest, I'm not surprised that Magnus had his assistant do his own job. The Treasurer always had the air of someone lazy and self-entitled.

"Good. Let me know if you need any help or assistance. Now that you're the acting Treasurer, you should probably have your own assistant. Do you have someone in mind?"

He nods enthusiastically. "My husband would be perfect for the job. He's had the same training I've had."

"Perfect. I'm sure Tamara will arrange his salary and contract."

The Mistress of the Household nods in approval and I turn to her, away from the new Treasurer.

"Tamara, how many Gods pledged their allegiance yesterday?"

She looks at her list. "Twenty-three, plus several other previous allies have confirmed that they'll be fighting on our side again. I'm waiting for more information from most of them, but if I take a rough guess, I'd say that we can now match Angus's numbers, if not beat them. We're still outnumbered if we add the Morrigan's demon army, but they're not as well trained and equipped as our Guardians. An Epona soldier, for example, can easily take ten demons."

"I'm feeling a lot more hopeful," Gwain admits. "This gives us the manpower to not only defend the Realms, but also to be on the offensive. We could attack Angus if you so command."

That sets me aback slightly. The whole time, we've been talking about defending the Realm, and now suddenly, there's a chance of us throwing the first metaphorical stone?

I'm not sure how I feel about that. Defending makes sense, there's no choice. If the people of this Realm are to survive, we have to take up arms and defend ourselves. But actively going into Angus's Realm and fighting him on his own lands... isn't that what he's doing to us?

"No, it isn't," Crispin whispers, so quietly that I'm the only one able to understand. He's taken Storm's seat in the Guardian's absence. "Think of what they did to us. What the Morrigan did to you. It's still defending, just not in our Realm."

"Are you reading my mind again?"

He shrugs. "Can't help it. It now seems to happen occasionally even when I don't touch you."

An issue for another time. As handy as it is to have him hear my thoughts in times of trouble, I really don't want him to be able to read my mind at all times. I don't have secrets from them, but my mind is mine and mine alone.

"Should we prepare our troops for a possible assault on the Summer Realm?" Gwain asks and the room falls completely silent. Everybody is staring at me.

My mother should be sitting in my place. It should be her making the decision.

So many lives could be lost.

Lives will be lost, no question about that. People I know and love could die.

Is it worth it?

A flash of light tears through my vision and I'm in Frost's head again. There's noise, so much noise, and smoke, and the smell of blood. He's lying on the ground, his legs twisted and hurting. Pain is fogging his thoughts, but he's clinging onto consciousness.

"Frost!" I shout, not sure if he'll be able to hear me. Maybe he's seeing the Council staring at him... me, rather than the dark stone corridor I see at the moment.

A shadowy figure bends down to me.

"I'm going to enjoy playing with you, sweetie."

That voice is familiar. So sweet and so poisonous at the same time. The Morrigan.

She's got Frost.

Suddenly, she's thrown to one side by a massive gust of wind. Storm! He's still fighting. That's good. I can't see Arc but hopefully, he's there as well.

"Can you stand?" Storm asks his brother but I shake my head. My legs hurt too much. They're broken, I'm sure of it. I need a healer... no, Frost does.

"Arc!" Storm shouts. "You carry the father, I carry Frost!"

The father. My father? My dad? They've got him?

"Not so fast," the Morrigan cackles, and it's the last thing I hear before I'm flung back into my own body, back in the Palace.

"Wyn?"

Someone is shaking me by the shoulders. "Wyn? Are you alright?"

My legs are tingling with Frost's pain. I need to help them.

"We need a distraction," I say into the quiet room. "Gwain, ready the troops. We're going to attack Angus. Tamara, Zephyr, let our allies know. Crispin, take twenty of our best fighters and travel to the Gate at Castle Tioram. They need a healer."

"How do you know...?" Gwain asks, bafflement clear in his voice.

"No time to explain. We need to act quickly, while the Morrigan is distracted. She isn't expecting an attack on Angus. If we manage to strike them both at the same time, they'll not be able to assist each other."

"Princess, it will take hours to get our army to the nearest Gate, let alone to the Summer Realm. We need to plan, we need time. Preparing an attack like that takes days."

I sigh. "Right now, in this very moment, three of my Guardians are fighting the Morrigan. They don't have a chance against her, but it's a distraction. They..."

What did I just say?

The truth.

She's a Goddess. They're three Guardians and one of them is wounded.

They're as good as dead.

They were never supposed to fight her. It was supposed to be a reconnaissance mission, with the hope that they might be able to free my dad.

They might be dead already.

Something shatters within me. My heart, maybe?

No, it's my magic. She's screaming, and I join her, screaming together as the heart cave around us crumbles, stalactites falling from the ceiling, stones crashing into the ground.

Blinding light is everywhere but I can't close my eyes. I stare as the cave that I thought was protection for my magic slowly collapses.

No, it wasn't protection. It was a prison.

The light increases, pouring into my magic. She's growing, from the size of a large house cat to that of a lion. Her screams become deeper as her voice changes. Her claws extend, each as sharp as diamonds. Her eyes are glowing brightly, watching in glee as the stone that was once her cave crumbles into dust.

She's free, and so am I.

I was never meant to be just a Demigoddess.

My magic takes a step towards me and I do the same, meeting her in the middle. I hug her tight.

We're no longer separate, our powers are merging, becoming what we were destined for.

We are one.

We are a Goddess.

Epilogue

Storm, two hours earlier

There's only about twenty demons guarding the Gate within the castle ruin and we dispatch them with ease. We're a practised team: Arc freezes a bunch of demons with his mind, my brother drowns them, I round up the others with gusts of wind to get the same treatment. Brutal, but effective. We don't have time to play nice today.

The Gate in front of us looks very different from the ones in the Winter Realm. Rather than the typical two standing stones covered by a large third stone slab, this one is a doorway that's part of the castle structure. It's a clever way to keep it from the attention of humans. Not that they can see the shimmer of magic covering the doorway like a spider's web, but standing stones attract tourists. Just look at Stonehenge, that Gate hasn't been used for a long time because it's been taken over by humans.

Frost wipes his bloody hands on his shirt.

"I hate demon blood," he complains. "It leaves stains."

"Have ye suddenly turned into Crisp?" Arc teases and Frost gives him an indignant glare.

"Stop the banter, we've got work to do," I admonish them and stride towards the Gate, leaving a pile of demon corpses behind. They follow and together, we step into the Morrigan's domain.

I've been in the Demon Realm before, many times, but this part of it seems unfamiliar. We're in a large cavern, illuminated by a glowing mould or moss covering the walls. There's nobody here. Strange. I had expected guards.

Slowly, we make our way through the cave, ready to fight at a moment's notice. The sound of our breathing echoes in the empty space, far too loud for my liking. The dark entrance to a tunnel looms up ahead and I point towards it, letting the others know our destination. The tunnel is completely dark, no glowing moss here to help us see what's waiting for us.

I extend my magic, looking for disturbances in the air. Someone is breathing not far from us, maybe fifty feet away. Only one though. Carefully, I wrap a wind lasso around them, and with a strong yank, pull them towards me. A demon flies through the air, landing heavily on the ground in front of me. It's a higher demon with four arms and a gaping maw. Surprisingly, it's not making a sound. Good for us, it means it won't alert any of its fellow demons.

Darkness swirls around him, its tendrils reaching out for us.

Before his magic can touch us, Frost slams a spear of ice into the demon's chest. He sinks back to the ground, twitching, before his body goes limp.

"That was too easy," Frost whispers, echoing my thoughts. Either the demons here have grown complacent, or this is a trap. I hope for the first. Maybe the Morrigan isn't here to keep them doing her bidding. She's enslaved them, so there's always the hope that they're fighting for her unwillingly. That would give us an advantage.

A trap is unlikely. Nobody knew we were coming here, except for Wyn, Gwain and Flora. I trust Gwain with my life, Flora has nothing to gain by betraying us, and Wyn... well, she's our Wyn. Enough said.

We make our way through the tunnel, with me checking for air disturbances every few minutes. There are no signs of life.

The tunnel never seems to end. It's too narrow for us to extend our wings, so we have to walk. Most demons can fly, so why wouldn't they have a better access route to the Gate? Maybe it was never intended as a Gate to be used for anything but an escape route. Maybe only the Morrigan uses it, who can teleport there in a flash.

We've been monitoring the other demon Gates, but we don't stop the demons from leaving or entering. That would be too much of a waste of resources. All we do is watch to see if larger groups of demons leave that might mean trouble. And more recently, our scouts have been looking out for the Morrigan and her allies. Not that they ever saw her – of course not, she has her own Gate in the middle of nowhere.

It takes us half an hour to reach the end of the tunnel.

"Finally," Arc whispers as a shimmer of light beckons in the distance. We increase our pace, glad to get out of this endless tunnel.

Just before we reach the end, I make them stop and extend my senses once again.

"Twenty demons up ahead," I say quietly. "Two of them are very large."

Arc cracks his knuckles and takes a large sword from his back.

"Let's have some fun," he roars before jumping out in the open, ready to hack at the demons waiting for us.

Frost grins and me and runs out as well, icicles flying from his hands, right into the chests of several demons. I join the fray, wrapping ropes of wind around the waists of two demons and ramming them into each other.

Blood paints the ground red as we kill the demons as quickly as possible. It only takes a minute to dispatch all of the demons, even the two big ones that are about twice my height.

We're good at killing; it's what we were made for.

"Where the fuck are we?" my brother asks, and I finally take in our surroundings. We're in another cavern, but this one is so large that I can't see where it ends. It could be several miles long, for all I know. The ceiling is so high that you could easily fit in some of the tallest towers of the Royal Palace.

More of the strange glowing moss is covering the walls, giving enough light to illuminate the massive fortress up ahead.

While the Palace in the Winter Realm is imposing and beautiful, this fortress feels threatening. The black stone shimmers unnaturally in the darkness and its jagged turrets seem to almost scratch the ceiling of the cavern. There are almost no windows, instead, small arrow slits are dotted around the walls. Two large ones above the main gate look like eyes staring into the distance, watching for intruders.

Basically, it's how most people would imagine a demon castle to look like.

"What are we going ta do, walk in through the front entrance?" Arc asks, looking at the fortress in disgust.

"Let's have a look around", Frost says, but I stop him.

"I have the darkest wings, let me."

His turquoise and Arc's copper wings would stand out too much, even in this darkness. My own are a dark blue, but in this light, they look black.

I jump into the air and fly towards the fortress, keeping close to the shadows. The closer I get, the more demons are down below. It seems like there are settlements at the foot of the castle, housing hundreds of demons. That definitely won't be the route we'll take.

Luckily, nobody spots me as I circle above them, looking for a way into the fortress. The back of the castle is built into the rock of the cavern, leaving three walls to search for an entrance.

Once, I get too close to a demon and he's about to cry out, but a quick burst of wind through his mouth and into his lungs stops him. He collapses, his lungs exploded.

I fly higher, hoping that there won't be barriers preventing us from flying into the fortress from above - but sadly, there are. Damn it. The bloody demons actually prepared for intruders. Maybe it's back from the times demons fought each other. I don't suppose they still do, now that they're all ruled by the Morrigan.

The wall closest to the tunnel we came through hasn't got a single door, neither does the one with the large gate. I'm starting to lose hope that we'll find an easy entrance, but then I spot a small crack in the third wall. I fly closer, curious.

The crack turns out to be a thin stone door that hasn't been closed properly. It's just around the corner from the large gate, a perfect way to surprise attacking forces and stop them from taking the gate. Right now, we're the invading force though, and this door will finally bring us closer to our goal.

I fly back to the others, killing three more demons on the way.

"There's a door," I tell them once I've landed, "but it's quite far from here. If we walk there, we'd have to get through several hordes of demons. Arc, if we fly, can you shield us from view?"

He nods. "Aye, but we need ta hurry, I dinnae want to use up too much energy."

"Good. I'll take you on the most direct route. If we get in trouble, you two fly to the door, I'll keep them off you."

They both nod grimly and extend their wings. I've always been a tad jealous of my brother's beautiful colours, but today, my darker ones are more practical.

I lead them to the door and surprisingly, we get there without incident. Arc's shielding seems to work. He once said that influencing demons' minds was much easier than manipulating humans or Guardians.

"Are you going to fit through there?" Frost asks Arc, the biggest of us.

"With a wee squeeze, aye," the Scot grumbles and takes the lead.

We sneak inside, progressing slowly through a maze of corridors. I dispatch of demons in our ways with my wind, while the other two are searching the rooms we pass for anything that could be useful. Our priority right now is to find weak spots in this fortress, and hopefully Wyn's father. As long as we don't encounter the Morrigan, we should be alright. These demons are easy prey, too surprised by our presence to resist much.

"Wait," Arc suddenly whispers. "There's a human below us."

He's been scanning our surroundings with his mind magic to give us some warning of any non-demons that may be lingering here.

"Is it her father?" I ask quickly and Arc closes his eyes in concentration.

"I dinnae ken, he's deeply unconscious. Or she, cannae even tell the gender."

"Okay, let's find a way down. There must be a staircase somewhere."

No, there isn't. After several rounds along the same corridors, it's clear that there are no stairs leading up or down from this floor.

"There has to be an exit besides the door we came through," my brother mutters. "It doesn't make sense."

"It has ta be concealed by magic," Arc suggests. "Maybe there's a draught of wind ye can feel, Storm?"

I sigh. "Let's walk around once more, I'll let you know if I notice something out of the ordinary."

We're almost back where we started when I finally feel a waft of air from my right, apparently coming from a solid wall. I stretch out a hand and touch the wall - except that there isn't one.

"Found it," I say drily and walk through the wall-that-isn't-a-wall.

We're in a circular staircase with stairs leading both up and down. We descend, ignoring several pathways leading away from the stairs until Arc tells us that we're on the floor he can sense the human on.

It's the dungeons. What a surprise. Rows of cells stretch out far into the darkness, their metal bars hiding things I don't want to see. It reeks of death and despair in here.

We walk along the corridor, Arc telling us all we need to know.

"Dead... dead.... dead... dead..."

He saves us from having to look into the cells. Some smell so strongly of decay that bodies must be rotting in there.

"... dead... alive!"

Arc breaks into a run, leading us to a cell no different from all the others.

Frost lays his fingers on the lock and freezes the metal until the door pops open.

As if the metal bars were an actual solid door, a terrible scent assails us as soon as we step into the cell. More rot and decay.

Two shapes are lying on the ground.

"Only the left one is alive," Arc mutters, his hands pressed over his mouth and nose to avoid breathing in the stench.

I summon a ball of light, making sure it only shines on the person on the left. I've seen my share of dead bodies, but I try not to if I can avoid it. Especially if the corpse is who I think it is.

I kneel by his side, rolling the man over to look at his face. Despite his shaggy beard, I recognise him. Wyn's father. There's a whole lot of dried blood on his temples and hairline, maybe that's why he's unconscious. I gently shake him, but he doesn't move at all.

"We need to carry him," I tell the others. "Frost, get him to the door and wait there for us. Arc and I will explore the upper floors. If we're not back in the next fifteen minutes, take him and pass through the Gate." My brother nods sharply. I expected him to argue, but in this moment, we're all professionals, not squabbling brothers.

Frost gently lifts up the man into his arms and we all leave the cells, glad to be away from the stench and the dead.

I t's an absolute waste of time. There is nothing in the rooms we explore that would give us an advantage. No documents, no plans, no maps. The fortress seems empty, almost unused, as if it's only one of many places the Morrigan occupies. She probably has her personal domicile further into the Demon Realm, where it's safer. She can teleport, so it doesn't matter how far away from the Gate she lives. Maybe this place is only used for keeping prisoners and as an oversized watchtower.

Disappointed, we make our way back to the door through which we entered the fortress.

"Stop," Arc says suddenly when we're only two corridors away. "Someone's there, with Frost."

Ignoring the fear slowly spreading in my chest, I send out my wind magic, exploring what's happening in the distance. Arc is right, there are several people by the door. Ten, at least.

"Ready?" I ask Arc and he nods grimly. "Let's take them down."

The demons waiting for us don't know what hit them as they crumple to the ground, crushed by the wind I conjured. Arc is sprinting ahead, letting me deal with the demons that are suddenly coming from all sides. There's definitely more than ten. It's like they've waited for us in the shadows, setting a trap we walked right into. Well, we didn't have a choice.

I can hear my brother scream at the other end of the corridor and I increase my pace, slashing into demons with my sword while killing others with my magic. It's slow progress, but I'm hoping that Arc has reached Frost by now.

Suddenly, a cackle fills the room, overpowering all the noise of fighting and demon wails.

I know that voice.

The Morrigan is here.

Fuck.

I create two whirlwinds, anchoring them to the walls, not letting anyone pass as I run towards her laughter. She's with Frost.

While I'm running, I conjure more wind, keeping the magic close to my chest, ready to throw it at my target.

The Morrigan is bent over my brother who's curled up on the floor. He's moving though, but he's too weak to escape her as her fingers trail over his shoulder.

"Get away from him!" I shout, flinging all the pent-up wind at her. She's thrown against one wall, her pretty face contorting in pain. Using more wind, I throw her down the corridor, away from us. I know I have no chance beating her, so keeping her off our backs is the only way we'll get out of here.

I let myself fall on my knees by my brother's side, gently touching his arm.

"Can you stand?" I ask him but he weakly shakes his head. I look down at his body and cringe at the unusual angle his legs are spread out. It must be fucking painful, I'm surprised he's not screaming.

Next to him lies the prone body of Wyn's dad, still unconscious.

"Arc!" I shout. "You carry the father, I carry Frost!"

I reach around Frost's shoulders, trying not to touch his legs too much. He groans when I lift him up, pain contorting his face.

"It'll be alright," I tell him, not quite believing it myself. "We'll get you to a healer as soon as we're out of here."

"Not so fast," the Morrigan cackles, suddenly back in front of us, appearing out of thin air. Why did Beira give that Goddess so many powers? It's making it very hard to fight her, let alone flee from her.

She stretches out her arms, fire circling around her wrists. Usually, Frost would be the one to protect us from fire, but he doesn't look like he's well enough to even notice what's going on.

I prepare some wind to throw at her in defence, but without warning, something strange happens. The magic inside of me *vibrates*, as if it's resonating to a sound from far, far away. I gasp as a warm feeling spreads through my body. It's a feeling of hope and love, something that reminds me of Wyn.

The Morrigan has stopped laughing and is swaying on her feet, her eyes unfocused. Frost must have seen the same thing because a second later, a large icicle is stuck in the Morrigan's chest. I stare at him in surprise; I didn't think he still had the energy for magic like that.

It's just in time to see his eyes flutter closed and his body go limp. Damn him, playing the hero. Now we have two unconscious men to carry.

Arc grabs Wyn's father and slings him over his shoulder, before we both start running, through the door into the open. Flying with Frost in my arms is hard; I'm having trouble keeping out of reach of the demons below. We're racing towards the Gate, hoping the Morrigan won't be able to catch up before we reach it.

Demons are shouting from beneath us, pointing up. Arc doesn't have the energy to both shield us from their view and carry Wyn's father. Hopefully, none of them will take to the air and pursue us.

Far too quickly, we need to land to enter the tunnel. I'm running as fast as I can, but I'm getting more tired with every step. There are a few bleeding wounds on my legs that I didn't even notice while the adrenaline of the fight was running through my veins, but now, they're making running painful.

It takes forever to reach the final cavern, and even longer to reach the Gate at its end. My legs are heavy and Frost keeps slipping from my grip. Arc isn't faring much better; he's breathing hard and cursing every few steps.

We stagger through the Gate, more falling than walking. I land on the wet ground, Frost still in my arms.

I sit up, expecting there to be demons, but the castle is deserted. Thank the Gods, we're not in the best shape to fight demons right now.

Suddenly, in a flash of light, figures appear all around us. Not demons though. Guardians. How the…

"Frost!" a very familiar voice shouts and a moment later, my brother is lifted from my arms. I'm too surprised to even protest.

I sit up and look around. Ten Guardians are standing around us in a circle, protectively facing out. We're safe.

Crispin is bent over my brother's body, his hands moving in complicated patterns. How did the healer get here? Thank the Gods that he is, though. My brother will be alright now, Crispin will fix his legs. I turn to search for Arc, who must have landed just behind me.

He's no longer holding his charge either. Wyn is.

Our Wyn.

She's cradling her father in her arms, her hands making the same movements that Crispin does when he's healing someone. Since when can she do that? Crisp showed her the mechanics of it all, but so far, she hasn't managed to heal even a tiny cut. Now it looks like she's mending her father's wounds.

"Wyn?" I ask hesitantly, and she looks up at me.

Her eyes are glowing bright blue, her features are sharper somehow and I'm sure that the hair on her head is her own and not a wig.

What the fuck happened to my Wyn?

~ The End ~

This was supposed to be the final book in the series, but well... the characters didn't like that. Wyn's story continues in Winter Goddess.

Subscribe to my newsletter for more books, offers and looks behind the scenes.
skyemackinnon.com/newsletter

About the Author

Skye MacKinnon is a USA Today & International Bestselling Author whose books are filled with strong heroines who don't have to choose.

She embraces her Scottishness with fantastical Scottish settings and a dash of mythology, no matter if she's writing about Celtic gods, cat shifters, or the streets of Edinburgh.

When she's not typing away at her favourite cafe, Skye loves dried mango, as much exotic tea as she can squeeze into her cupboards, and being covered in pet hair by her tiny demonic cat.

Subscribe to her newsletter:
skyemackinnon.com/newsletter

facebook.com/skyemackinnonauthor

twitter.com/skye_mackinnon

instagram.com/skyemackinnonauthor

bookbub.com/authors/skye-mackinnon

goodreads.com/SkyeMacKinnon

Also By

Find all of Skye's books on her website, **skyemackinnon.com**, where you can also order signed paperbacks.

Many of her books are also available as audiobooks.

Claiming Her Bears (Post-apocalyptic bear shifter RH)

Rescued by Bears

Protected by Bears

Craved by Bears

>> Box set

Infernal Descent (paranormal RH based on Dante's Inferno, co-written with Bea Paige)

Hell's Calling

Hell's Weeping

Hell's Burning

>> Box set

Seven Wardens (Paranormal RH co-written with Laura Greenwood)

From the Deeps

Into the Mists

Beneath the Earth

Within the Flames

Above the Waves

Under the Ice

Rule the Dark

Prequel: Beyond the Loch

Spin-off: Through the Storms

>> Box set (books 1-4)

>> Box set (books 5-7)

The Lost Siren (post-apocalyptic, paranormal RH co-written with Liza Street)

Song of Blood

Lullaby of Death

Melody of Souls

Starlight Highlanders Mail Order Brides (m/f alien romance, part of the Intergalactic Dating Agency)

Thorrn

Eron

Cyle

Between Rebels (sci-fi RH set in the Planet Athion shared world)

Stolen By Them

Guarded By Them

Chosen By Them

>> Box Set

The Intergalactic Guide to Humans (sci-fi romance, RH, m/f and fmf)

Alien Abduction for Beginners

Alien Abduction for Professionals

Alien Abduction for Experts

Alien Abduction for Pirates

Alien Abduction for Santa

The Mars Diaries (Sci-fi RH linked to the Claiming Her Bears series)

Alone

Hidden

Found

>> Box Set

Through the Gates (dystopian RH co-written with Rebecca Royce)

Purgatory City

Defiance (contemporary dark RH)

Frozen Heart

Loving Heart

Broken Spirit

Stolen Soul

Academy of Time (time travel academy standalones)

Taking Her Vikings

Exploring Her Professor

Saving His Queen

Catnip Assassins (urban fantasy reverse harem)

Meow

Scratch

Purrr

Hisss

Lick

Claw

Roar

Thud (Christmas special)

>> Box set Books 1-4

>> Box set Books 5-7

>> Box set Books 1-7

Aliens and Animals (sci-fi romance co-written with Arizona Tape)

The Alien's Zookeeper

The Alien's Veterinarian

Standalones

Song of Souls – fairy tale retelling

Cupid's Apprentice - paranormal RH

Storm Witch - historical paranormal RH

Their Hybrid – steampunk RH

Partridge in the P.E.A.R. - sci-fi RH co-written with Arizona Tape

Highland Butterflies – lesbian romance

Anthologies and Box Sets

Hungry for More – charity cookbook

Daggers & Destiny – a Skye MacKinnon starter library